DREAM OF A NEW LIFE

Melanie Evans

CONTENTS

CHAPTER 1

Alara: I wonder what would happen if I got caught. When the plates food stop showing up in the afternoon, my mother might think I've given up and abandoned her.

Brilliant jewels and lanterns shine like an ocean of colour and light. I used to know this life; I used to be a part of it. But that was a long time ago, and there is no time for reminiscing when hunger is eating a hole in my stomach.

Nobody notices me in the bustle of the souk. My rags blend into the stained brown bags of rice and salt. It's easier this way, to not be noticed. Safer.

Soft flute music floats through the air along with the playful laughter of children trying to catch each other, their parents shouting after them to slow down.

Everything is different here in Quadura. The air smells like aromatic spices instead of raw fish. The ground is layered in cobblestone instead of sand. If these people, coated in their luxurious shawls and thobes, were to step foot in Wadi, their clothes would be stolen right off their backs.

The glimmer of light on a ruby-studded bracelet catches my eye. In the sun, the inclusions of the gem make the bracelet chatoyant. It will be enough to feed mama and I for over a month, if any merchant will trade with me tomorrow.

Attached to the bracelet is a woman embellished in jewels of emerald, jade and even pearls. Her skin is fair, from not having to do labour out in the sun. I doubt she'll miss a bracelet that she could most probably replace with the flick of her wrist.

I step up beside her, pretending to admire the most intricate silver lace brocaded slippers displayed in the stall. My feet will never find their way into something so beautiful.

I assess the clasp of the bracelet as she hands a purse heavy with coin to the merchant. His eyes wrinkle with joy at the sight of it. "Shukran," he repeats over-and-over, until she is turning away to find more unnecessary items to buy.

I step forward, ready to brush against her and slip the bracelet off without hesitation.

Before I get the chance, an intimidating figure in a hooded garb, shifts her out the way and grabs my wrist with force. His face is hidden in the shadows of his hood. The attire he wears is maroon and lined with gold, the colours of royalty. If he is part of the royal guard, I am never going to see my mama again. "What are you doing?" His voice is deep and rough, like the low growl of a hungry animal.

My heart lifts up into my throat, making it impossible to speak. His fingers tighten around my wrist, and he drags me into a dark corner. He stands tall, his body towering over me. The hint of a dagger can be seen beneath his clothes.

Nobody can see us here. If he were to shove my limp body into a potato sack, nobody would notice. I wonder if my mom would try to look for me; if she would get off the sofa for her daughter.

"What do you want?" I ask, my voice barely audible. I try to pull out of his forceful grip, but he doesn't release me, knowing I'll run.

"That's a dangerous question." He uses his free hand to tip his hood back. His desert brown eyes trail over me. He won't touch me, not when I'm wearing rags and have soot coated in my skin and hair.

His olive skin is smooth and clean. His beard is groomed closely against his strong jaw. Not the signs of a royal guard, but of a—

His face shifts closer to my ear. The strong, earthy scent of oud hugs me. "If you're going to steal, don't ever get caught." He holds out the ruby-studded bracelet between his index finger and his thumb. It looks tiny in his grip. My stomach does a somersault, making me feel nauseous. "Tell me, what will you do with it?"

My eyes fall to the bracelet. It's colours are muted in the shadows. I'm not sure if it's worth the vulnerablility of the truth because, in a world like this, having someone you care for is dangerous. "Feed my mama." Fear is stopping me from forming correct sentences. My Abu would be disappointed.

He opens my hand and drops the ruby bracelet onto my palm. The piece is cool against my skin. His lips turn up at the corners as he finally releases my wrist.

I push away from him, and sprint through the souk, tucking the bracelet into the pouch on my waist. My shoulders brush against blue of people passing through. They reprimand me for my rude manners, but I don't look back until my lungs are burning and my legs are aching with fatigue.

My fingers wrap around my wrist, mimicking the stranger's action. I've never seen anyone so well groomed, even here in Qadura.

Shaking my head, I pick up my pace and follow my usual trail through the narrow pathways that weave between the large, stone mansions. Fairy lights are strung up overhead. I imagine they must be beautiful when turned on at dusk, but I would never risk being out here that late, not after hearing the stories of Jazaar—the slaughterer.

I reach the mountain peaks that seperate Qadura and Wadi. My Abu, my father, always taught me to persue intelligence instead of beauty. Most traders and merchants wanting to cross between the two lands have to go around the mountain, but I have found a way to go through it.

The sun scorches the stone, making it impossible to climb. I wrap my hands in the cloth that was tucked in my waistband and begin the ascent up the rocky terrain.

Near the top of the peak, a small arch is carved directly through the mountainside. The inside has begun to wither, the roof engraved with strange marks, hidden by moss and dirt.

The air smells damp with age and lack of sunlight. The further in I step, the darker it becomes, until I have to trail my fingers along the rugged stone walls for guidance. Sometimes the darkness can be a tranquil escape, because it allows me to imagine myself having more than the life I am living.

A day where I might be able to wake up late in the morning, and do nothing but read books and sip on camomile tea. Maybe my home will be hidden up in a canopy of trees in Ardifa, or carved into the mountains north of Qadura.

A girl can dream. At least until I step out the other end of the mountain, into the air that seems to suffocate me. It is warm and arid, the sun baking my skin from the inside out. The view is barren, aside from the tan brown sand and cramped, unfinished houses.

The only thing of value here in Wadi was deemed of value by the people of Qadura. Uncoincidentally, it is also the only thing that has been fully constructed here. The Docks. It is where I will be going tomorrow, to barter the ruby bracelet for whatever I can get. Mama will be so happy—or maybe happy is a push. She hasn't been happy in years. I hope she will smile.

I unravel the cloths from my hands and use them to cover my hair. Being covered makes me feel safer; makes me feel like nobody is looking at me.

My head dips as I slip into the shadows of the homes, hiding from the blistering sun. My skin becomes sticky from the heat.

Many of the houses I pass are made from scraps or mud. They smell of waste and mildew. Clothing hangs from the holes in the walls, made as make-shift windows for light during the day.

Curiousity gets the best of me when I pass a home where the 'windows' are cut too low into the tin walls of the house. Inside, a family sits on a rug eating a meal and laughing together. An older lady presses a kiss to her child's temple as she hands him his bowl of food. The sight warms my heart. Even when the people of Wadi have nothing, they find something to be grateful for.

I reach my home. The sight of it makes my chest feel like it is caving in, the way the roof is. In a way, mama and I are lucky, because her cousin gave her this place—and it has a tap, which is more than most people have. Many come by to use it.

Inside, the dishes are unwashed beside a black bucket on the floor. My eyes adjust to the dull, grey lighting. The air trapped in here is stagnant and filled with dust. Mama sleeps on a small couch in the left corner of the room, her body hidden beneath a thin, fraying blanket. The space is mostly empty, because we sold what Abu left us for food.

Untying my pouch from my waist, I slip it underneath the mat that I sleep on. I'll take it out tomorrow, to barter the piece of jewellery.

I kneel beside my mama's sleeping form and gently brush the back of my fingers against her cheek. Her skin has softened with age. I was made in her image; kinky curls, cocoa brown eyes, and as short as a childrens book. Her face is serene when she's asleep, and filled with worry and unending sadness when she is awake.

I love her with all of my heart, because when my Abu left, she could have abandoned me. It would have made things a lot easier, not having a six-year-old to feed.

Her eyes flutter open for a moment. "Habibi?" Her voice is hoarse and broken. Habibi. That used to be a word that rep-resented love. It was what she called my Abu. Now that word reminds me that love has never mattered. The only thing that matters is survival. I've got your back.

CHAPTER 2

Z ayen: The greatest burden left on a man is the burden of living after killing.

It was not by choice. It was for the man sitting at the low wooden table in the center of the room, chewing on the bones of a roasted chicken. The loud crunching echoes through the silent room.

The table is filled with food. Ignorant men sit on patterned cushions around the table, quietly awaiting a word from the Hakeem, the ruler of these lands. They are like little kilaab—dogs—ready to tend to Hakeem Barak's every need.

They should be eating, yet they do not know that every morsel of food left uneaten will be thrown out. Not given to the servants or the poor, but carelessly and purposefully discarded.

The Hakeem chooses not to feed the hungry. He is only kind to those who can give him something in return. But nobody knows this. They see the dazzling smile and the free flowing drinks and believe him to be generous.

The low hiss and crackle of the flames trapped in lanterns around the room is the only thing that keeps me grounded and stops me from shoving a scimitar through the Hakeem's back.

My hand stays on my weapon; my eyes stay on anything except the excuses of men in this room.

The lanterns make the gold and wooden furniture glow. Sheer curtains dance against the warm evening air blowing in. Large arches open up to the rest of the palace, where the high ceilings are engraved with patterns and intricate details.

Footsteps brush against the polished stone floors, and Nawaz appears beneath one of the large arches. There is not a single crease in his clothes, almost like he stands perfectly still and does absolutely nothing the entire day. He is flanked by two guards, including my best friend Ali.

"You called for me?" Nawaz asks, breaking the silence in the room. He is the Hakeem's son. The alleged heir.

The best way to describe Nawaz is to imagine a bolt of lightening that was converted into human form. He is mesmerising and bright from afar, but get too close and you'll never know what hit you.

"Yes, I called you to discuss the ma'duba tomorrow night. I will bring women for you to choose from," the Hakeem says, his voice low and firm.

He is always strategic and concise with every move he makes, and every word he speaks. He expects the same for his son—starting with a marriage of convenience.

Nawaz is being instructed to choose a wife, but when his father offers him the most beautiful and wealthy women on a platter, all he does is pick them up and spit them out like grape seeds.

I take Nawaz's arrival as my chance to escape. On my way out, Ali flares his nose at me and I have to purse my lips to not smile at him.

We have made the mistake of joking around while on duty, and we were beaten for it. Seeing the regret in Ali's eyes for making me laugh caused a deeper pain than the bruises left behind—but, to this day, it has never stopped him from being an idiotic clown.

I take the steep steps down into the guard's quarters. The air at the bottom is bone dry and feels as if it is feeding off of my skin. At the end of the dark hallway stands a large wooden door guarded by two men, and behind it is the aleamiq—a hell of a prison. The wails of men and woman in ceaseless pain can be heard throughout the night, most of them innocent of everything except displeasing the Hakeem.

I step off to the left, into my quarters. It is a cramped space, enough to fit a single flat mattress and a cupboard. Because it is underground, there is no light or windows, aside from the two dying lanterns fitted into the walls. The bathrooms are shared between guards, and it made me realise how many people lack basic hygiene and cleanliness. Most of the toilet seats are splattered with liquid and, occasionally, pubic hair.

Lowering myself onto my bed, I lean my arms behind my head and wait for my punishment. Nawaz has no doubt given his favoured guards their orders. He always does, and they always follow through.

The stagnant air wraps around me like a suffocating blanket. It almost lulls me to sleep, but I refuse to let my eyes fall closed.

Right on time, the rotting door to my room swings open with a loud thud, and three men in the same attire as me—black harem pants and a top, with their weapons attached to them like second skin—barge in and roughly try to grab me. It takes all three of them to pull me off the bed, which makes me smile internally.

The shortest and bulkiest of the three swings a punch into my stomach, right below my ribs. My body hunches over, a pained groan leaving my lips. I've stopped trying to fight back, not for a lack of ability, but because I just want it to be over with.

"Good shot. I wonder if you only punch my stomach because you can't reach any higher." I smirk arrogantly. The amount of punches do not determine who comes out the winner. It's the man who can stand tall at the end of it that wins.

As predicted, because it happens every time, his face reddens and he elbows me in the ribs. Then he waddles out and leaves me with the other two, who are not as easy to shake off.

Khalid, an old friend that grew up beside me and trained with me, grabs me by the hair and knocks me down to my knees. Money and power changes people.

The other guard, who is new and unfamiliar, cracks his knuckles. There's a sly smile on his face as he throws his first punch into my ribs. It is followed by several more in my stomach and chest. Each hit seems to feel like a lead block falling onto me. It leaves a deep ache in my bones that will stay for days.

I turn my head to spit blood onto the floor and then take a deep breath, preparing for more. I've realised that when I don't fight back, they get bored faster.

Nawaz always does this. He is not going to stop any time soon. He instructs them to avoid my face, in case his father sees.

The Hakeem took one look at young Nawaz, who had the same green eyes as him, and said 'that is my son'.

It didn't matter that I was his son first.

CHAPTER 3

Alana: Money is a disastrous thing. It causes people to do things that they would have never imagined themselves doing.

Dressing up as royalty to sell a bracelet is something I never imagined myself doing, yet here I am.

The pathway leading to end of the docks, where traders and merchants set up a huge tent every Friday after Jummah, seems to go on forever. In reality it is only a minutes walk.

Every step forward tightens the fist around my heart, squeezing until my head is light and my breath is short.

Guards with weapons at their sides and readiness in their gazes patrol the area, making sure no 'unworthy' Wadi's try and touch the people here. I'm sure they would kill someone like me without hesitation. Here, a life with no money is a life of no value.

I've traded before, but never with a piece like the one wrapped in the small purse hanging at my waist. Only the upper class and royalty can trade here. If I am caught, I don't think there is going to be a handsome stranger to save my back a second time.

The intolerable heat of the afternoon and the putrid smell of fish doesn't go away, no matter who shows up here in Wadi.

I wipe the perspiration from my forehead and step through the flaps of the tent and into the decorated space. It is lined with wooden stalls that must have been brought in only an hour ago. Unlike the souk in Qadura, everyone here is quiet and poised. The only sounds comes from the band playing stringed instruments at the back of the tent.

There are merchants and traders from all over Ahlam, here to make extra coin from the wealthiest people in Diyar and Qadura. Men and women stand behind the stalls, covered by mountains of spices, rugs or aged books. A few stalls sell mouth-watering foods and desserts, all freshly made. It makes my stomach twist with hunger.

The floors are temporarily covered with maroon rugs. I roll my eyes at the pageantry. I guess only servant and lower class walk on wood.

Walking past each stall, I make sure to hold my chin high and keep my shoulders back. My Abu made sure I was educated when I was young; he hired tutors who taught me nearly everything, including communication which comes majorly from the way someone carries themselves.

There is a jewellery trader near the back of the tent. She speaks with a broad-shouldered man that stands tall with pride. From the arrogance on his aged face, he must think he is made of gold. His shoes are studded with gems that sparkle with every movement of his feet.

The bracelet will blend in perfectly here. The jewellery trader's stall displays the most beautiful and delicate gems. Some are designed into pendants that sit on small chains, others sit alone as engraved and chiselled pieces. With every movement of my eyes, the light inside each gem shifts, creating a moving masterpiece. This woman is not here to mess around.

I step forward and drop the purse in front of her. It lands with a gentle jingle. Neither am I.

The trader, her hair wrapped up in a pink scarf, drags her eyes away from the arrogant-looking man. Her features are gentle, but her eyes are fierce as she assess me.

When she sees my attire—an emerald green silk dress—she glances down at my purse. This dress is the only thing of value that I own. It was gifted to my mother before I was born, and she instructed me to sell it for food, but I chose to keep it. It is a treasure to me; something to remember life isn't all bad.

The trader gently opens the purse and tips the stolen piece onto her open palm. Along with the other gems in her stall, the ruby gleams and glitters.

"Where did you get a piece like that, girl?" The man with fancy shoes questions me. His voice is firm and holds a sense of power. He must be royalty, but he wears no symbols of royalty—no kiffyeh or royal colours or weapons engraved with royal markings.

Then again, I don't wear any either. He might be a fake, just like me.

In order for my act to be believable, I tilt my head and glower at him. "It was a gift. And don't call me girl."

"Then what should I call you?"

Panic surrounds me. I keep my feet rooted to the ground. Avoiding shifting and fidgeting will help me come off as confident. Squaring my shoulders, I say, "I am a relative of the royal house of Diyar." It is a safer bet to claim relation to Diyar, since it is further away and he may not know of anyone from there.

"What do you want to trade for this?" the woman questions. She eyes the jewel and, from the spark in her eyes that she tries to conceal, I know she wants it.

"One hundred coins." It is asking for a lot, but it is a fair price. I tilt my head and watch her for any reaction.

She gives none, except the slightest nod of her head. "Eighty."

That is way more than I expected to walk out of here with. It would feed me and my mama for three months or more.

In the mean time, I could get a job and save up for a better home or—

"Wait," the older man asks. I want to grab the purse of eighty coins from the woman and run, because I'm so close. "What do you plan to do with the money?" His assessing eyes watch me, reminding me of the eyes of a serpent.

"Who are you to question me?" I ask. My tone is cutting. I need to act as if I would shout 'off with his head!' or whatever royal people do in their free time.

He keeps his mouth shut. I'd assume most royals would be quick to give out their titles and how much power they have. His silence holds much more weight.

Before I can turn back to the woman, the jingle of coins comes from the strange man and he holds out the bag to me. "One hundred coins. If you can attend tonight's ma'duba and court my son, I will add an extra four hundred." A ma'duba is a formal banquet attended by the wealthiest people in all four cities.

I almost do not want to ask. "Who is your son?"

"Nawaz ibn Barak." The crowned prince of Qadura. At the mention of his son, his posture shifts and a smile tugs at his lips, causing wrinkles at the corners of his eyes. He now carries a different kind of pride to the one he held when I first laid eyes on him—the pride of a father.

"I . . ." My head is shaking no before my lips are saying it. There is no ways I could court a prince. That is the stuff that happens in fairytales, to girls who are honest and honourable. I am neither of those.

He tells me to listen. "Estme' lee, you do not have to respond. Take some time, consider it, and if you choose to come then you could make more money to do whatever you planned to do with that eighty." It sounds too good to be true. He turns and walks off, his silk thobe subtly reflecting the lights inside the tent.

"Do you still want to sell this bracelet?" The woman asks.

There is no way I could return it to that lady I took it from. "Yes, shukran." I could give the coins to someone else in Wadi. There is no shortage of people desperate for even a single coin.

She pushes the bag of coins towards me, and I lift it. The weight of the second purse in my arms makes me feel wary. How could I walk around with this amount in Wadi? I am so screwed.

Chapter 4

Zayen: Two figures sit in the corner of the dark room, cuddled together. Their forms are so small that they'd be invisible if I didn't know exactly where to look—in the same spot I always find them each day before dawn.

The matchstick roars to life between my fingers and send a small trail of smoke up into the air. I light the candles that sit around the room. They're usually unlit, even though I have told Saad and Aya to light them when they come in.

As soon as the candlelight reveals my face, they jump to their feet and run up to me, holding their hands up for me to carry them. Instead of lifting them, I get down on my knees and pull them both into a tight hug. Aya's soft giggles reverberate against me. My eyes fall closed and I pull them in tight.

I fear a day will come where they won't be here, in the dark corner, waiting excitedly to see me.

"Shh," Saad chastises. His tiny finger lifts to his lips, his brows scrunching. For someone who is only nine years old, he is such a grandfather.

I grin and ruffle his hair and he beams at me. Aya's adorable, tiny hand grips onto my bicep and she pinches me.

"Laa, Aya. We don't pinch our friends, okay?"

"Mamam?" Her voice is a gentle melody.

"It's not mamam, it's food." Saad shakes his head at her.

I chuckle. "That's right, boss." I point to the brown paper bag by the door, and before I can stand up, Aya is running to the bag. She tears it open and the contents fall to the floor.

Kids are a handful. Especially when they have no parents to teach them right from wrong.

"Hey, don't tear the packet." I walk over to her, a sigh leaving my lips. The bruises on my ribs ache as I bend to pick up the fruit and loaves of bread from the dusty floor. "You see, now your food is getting dirty. Say sorry to your brother for dirtying his food."

"Sorry Saaaaad," she says, her chin tucking against her chest. Her eyelashes brush against her cheek as she stares at the floor like a hurt puppy.

"Now sit down and fold your legs." They follow my instructions, sitting side by side, knees touching. I dust off the food, tearing off the pieces of bread that might be too dirty to eat, and hand the salvageable food to them.

Footsteps outside the darkened room silence all three of us. Boots crunch against the stones and my eyes fall closed. The terror on their faces break me, because I want to destroy everything that they fear. But I can't.

Children shouldn't know what it feels like to be scared for their lives.

The idea of the Hakeem or one of Nawaz's guards catching them near the palace leaves a twisting sensation in my stomach. I've seen what they are capable of; I know they don't care because they don't have to explain themselves to anyone.

The footsteps stop, elevating my heart rate. My hands go to the dagger tucked into my pants and I pull it out, holding it at my side.

They might not be my children, they might not be my blood at all, but I would still give my life for them. When Saad dragged his baby sister to me, so tiny and weak that she could barely breathe properly, I couldn't turn them away. My heart immediately latched onto them, and has never let go.

Aya begins to sob, her lip quivering. I kneel down and hold the handle of my dagger out to her. The gems attached to it shine and reflect in the candle light—purples, reds and greens. She sniffles and stares at it with wide eyes, then reaches out to wrap her hand around the handle that is too big.

She tries to tug it out of my hand and it cuts my finger. I clench my jaw and turn to the door to listen for more footsteps, but they're gone.

"Aya, you see, you hurt me." I hold out my finger. A small line of blood is beginning to swell.

Her mouth forms an 'O' and she sucks in a breath of air. "Sorry, ba." Her voice is barely a whisper. She pulls my hand closer and inspects it. "Kiss?"

I smile. She learnt that from me. If she ever gets hurt, I kiss it better.

It was stupid of me to bring a dagger anywhere near a three-year-old child, but if she started to cry, her fate would have been worse than any harm a small dagger could cause.

"Finish eating. You need to go before the sun comes up," I say. Aya picks up the bread and starts chewing, but Saad obstinately refuses and sits with his arms folded. I sigh. "What?"

"I don't want to go."

I sit beside him and fold my legs, pulling his small body into my side. Beside him, I feel like a giant. "I know, but we can't risk it. You know that there will be guards everywhere soon."

He leans against me and his eyes fall closed. My heart tightens. All this kid wants is love—how could I deny him that?

But I can't be soft. Their safety is in my hands, so I will stay strong. For them. They'll understand one day, I hope.

"Did you do your reading?" I ruffle his short curls. He cuts his own hair, quite terribly, but that is how he will learn.

Unfortunately for Aya, he cuts her hair too. I've tried to stop it, but once in a while they show up looking like cavemen and it's too late for me to do anything.

His eyes light up. "I did all five pages!" He holds out a hand, displaying five small fingers.

I cup his face in my hand and brush my thumb against his soft cheek. I am so proud of him. When I met him, he couldn't even read. Now when he gets a book in his hands, he will not let it go until he gets the words right. "Well done, kid."

Aya comes and sits on my lap, causing a putrid smell to fill my nose. My least favourite part—that is why I reassigned it.

"Aya needs a nappy change. Let's see how you do it." I know, it's not ideal to make a nine-year-old change a diaper, but there are worse things in this world. Plus, he has to be there for her when I am not.

He hops up, ever willing to prove himself, and grabs the small backpack that he carried with.

The majority of it is filled with random scraps that he tried to turn into artwork. It seems like most of it got crumpled in the bag.

Finally, he pulls out a nappy from the bottom of the bag and sets it in the floor. "Linunazif, Aya." Let's clean. She starts walking in the opposite direction, giggling. "One . . ."

She swivels and smiles at him, her two front teeth missing. "Ba, no!"

"Two . . ." See, like a grandfather.

She starts waddling towards him and sits in front of him, letting him change her nappy.

He finishes up and pulls her pants back on. When they grow up, there is going to be nothing in the world stronger than their bond.

"Well—" The deep, reverberating sound of a horn being blown rattles through the room. That is a signal that the night shift is swapping out for the morning shift. "Time to go."

Saad shifts his backpack over his shoulders and holds onto the straps, looking up at me and waiting for me to lead.

"I'm sorry, kid, but I have to work the morning shift today. You'll have to go through the mountain on your own, okay?"

He nods, his gaze falling to the floor. He's disappointed but he won't admit it. "Tomorrow?" His voice is softer now, unsure.

I lean down and wrap my arms around him, lifting him up into my arms. His eyes immediately fill with that sparkle that I love. "Tomorrow."

One day they will get to stay with me, and they won't have to leave before the sun rises. One day, they will have a good life. I oath on it.

CHAPTER 5

Alara: Our neighbour, Abbas, usually comes by to use the water from our tap. When he came yesterday, I gave him half of the money I received from the market and promised him that he would get the other half if he takes care of my mother until I return. He wouldn't take anything less than everything I have, but if I fail with the prince I think I can reason with him to leave some for me.

It is risky asking a seventy-year-old man to take care of my sick mother, but he is someone that I trust to not take advantage of the situation and to stay true on his word.

A camel walks past me, it's hooves clicking against the ground, forcing me to move aside as I stare up at the palace. There are no gates—probably because there are enough guards to surround the area anyways.

I've been into Qadura before, but I have never been this close to the palace. I never risk stealing this close, not when there are eyes everywhere.

The palace itself is breathtaking. Tan coloured minarets, covered in Islamic engravings, rise up into the skies. The domes are framed by the soft hues of the sunset.

I used to have a stupid, recurring thought that I might come and find my father here—like in the stories. But I am no princess. That much I am sure of.

I force one foot in front of the other until I am crossing the bridge towards the palace. Guards line each side of the bridge, their eyes all on me. I am sure nobody dares to show up late for a royal ma'duba.

Still, I keep my chin tilted up and my shoulders back. I've been to the trading at the port in Wadi enough times to know that royalty treat their guards and servants like dirt.

I refuse to do that, but I can avoid eye contact. Mostly because if I look at them I might spill my guts.

The entrance to the palace is an archway that has repeated smaller arches going in, each smaller arch contains new engravings and designs. It is mind blowing.

Inside, there are gigantic passageways which surround a indoor garden. The ceilings are all engraved with designs telling an unknown story.

I trail my fingers along the smooth wall, my eyes wide with wonder. Na'am, I can do this. Several glassless window arches look out into the garden that is filled with lush greenery and flowers. In the setting sun, the colours become something only found in a gentle dream.

"It's beautiful, isn't it?" A deep voice says from behind me. The stranger's voice is rough, yet soothing. It suits this place.

"I can't imagine how long it must have taken to build this." The walls are made of bricked stone. But the engravings, it had to have taken centuries.

I know I should be looking at the stranger I am talking to. It's rule number one of manners that people of royalty should possess, but I can't look away from the design of this place. "Living here must be incredible."

"Most days the halls are silent and void," he chimes in.

"Exactly. You could sit in the garden and read, or do absolutely nothing. What a luxury."

"It's only a luxury for a week, maybe two, until you get bored and itch for more. Or until you realise that people out there are starving and dying while you sit in a pompous little garden."

"Pompous?" A strange half-laugh sound leaves my lips as I turn to assess the strange man with his unusual point of view. My beating heart stills. "You."

Without being covered by his garb, the sharpness of his cheekbones and the precision on his beard stands out. It's intimidating.

He looks down at his clothing, the attire of the guards here. A pair of plain black harem pants and a tight linen shirt. "I knew I looked good, but I didn't think I'd take your breath away like this." His voice is rough.

It shows a lot of confidence that the palace guards do not wear armour.

Those soft eyes, like sands shifting in the desert, trail over me. "Wow, thievery sure does pay well." My eyes widen and I glance around the empty hallways. "Relax, everyone is inside the hall kissing the Hakeem's feet."

I step closer, trying to keep it together. "You talk a lot more than I imagined you would." Before, he was just the silent hero, now he is the flirty guard with my life in his hands.

"If I wasn't talking when you imagined me, what was I doing?" A smirk tilts one side of his lips upwards.

"Walking away." His smirk falls, making me straighten my shoulders and turn, hoping I am heading towards the right direction. Music and lights flood out of a pointed archway, along with the voices of too many people.

Two lowered tables sit in the centre of the hall, surrounded by plush pillows. Each pillow has a mandala design intricately weaved into it. Lanterns line the walls and candles are laid wherever there is a gap not filled with mouth watering food.

It smells of expensive spices and warm bread. My stomach immediately twists at the amount of food. If anyone knows how to live in excess, it's the rich and powerful.

The kids in Wadi, the camps in Ardifa. There is so much food and wasted money here that could be given to—Stop. I don't want my thoughts to be written on my face. Not when I need to be thinking like royalty.

If only I had any idea how royalty think.

"If you want to fit in here, dish out more than you can eat and praise the Hakeem with compliments." His voice brushes against my ear. I suck in a breath at the sensation. He's so close.

I turn to thank him—the guard with the unknown name—but he's gone, faceless among the countless people in here.

My eyes shift over the crowd. Everyone is dressed in fine gowns and gold lined outfits. Instead of finding the guard, I find the Hakeem. He is standing near the head of the table, embellished in a white robe. A matching white kiffyeh sits on top of his head, held in place with a black ring. His smile is dazzling as he grips onto the man he speaks to.

He seems to charm the people that he speaks to. Something has shifted in him. His shoulders are still straightened with pride but his manner is more open and welcoming.

I gravitate towards him, each step making me feel like I need to run into that beautiful garden and throw up.

The Hakeem's eyes fall on me, as well as the eyes of the man he was talking to before. Power emanates from both of them. It makes me wish the floor would turn into a puddle of quick sand. I have never been this close to people of royalty—only at a distance in the Jummah market. "Remind me of your name, girl." Girl.

I can't give away my real name. It might lead this man back to my mother. I will never put her in danger. Not for my lies. What is a name I've always found beautiful? "Malaika."

"Your full name, Malaika?"

"I don't share my full name, for safety reasons." When it comes to lies, sharing less makes things easier.

He turns and assesses the people in the room. I shift backwards, wondering if that is how he declares the conversation over. Until his voice booms over the music, making me jump. "Nawaz!"

The prince. I know this was the plan, but I don't feel ready. If one thing goes wrong, I will lose all of the money I was promised. The money I gave to our neighbour, Abbas, to take care of my mother is no longer mine, so if I fail here I will be back to square one with absolutely nothing.

Having nothing to lose has it's benefits, but it gets exhausting sometimes. All I need is to make a good impression. I'm willing to do anything to get this money, it will allow me to finally buy a home for my mother. A bed. She would love a bed.

I will give my soul to see her smile again.

"Meet Malaika, from the royal family of Diyar." The Hakeem's voice pulls me out of my state of panic.

The prince. Right in front of me. His light green eyes are on me, trailing up from my sandals to my dress to my eyes. I don't miss how he takes his time assessing fit of my dress to my waist and chest.

I bought a new dress for tonight, with some of the money I kept aside, before giving the rest to Abbas. The Hakeem might find it questionable if I wore the same dress he saw me in on Friday.

This dress is the deepest shade of blood. It contrasts against my skin. Worthy of winning over a prince.

"Marhaba, Malaika," he greets. The way he says the name makes me wish it was mine. His smile is a replica of his fathers. Charming, friendly and hiding many things.

"Hi," I whisper, suddenly breathless. Black ink runs up from his hands to beneath the rolled up sleeves of his button down shirt. I've never seen markings like this on someone before.

"I can show you the rest of you'd like, but I'd have to start taking of my clothes for that." A player. He has most likely said those words a thousand times.

Yet my cheeks still heat up. "Oh, uh, no." I search for the Hakeem, but he is gone. I'd much rather go hide in a dark corner than speak to anyone here, but my job is to 'woo' the prince. "I mean . . . When?" It feels like something is trapped in my throat.

He nods his head towards a door that is at the back of the room. "Follow me." He walks ahead of me, not bothering to look back and check if I am coming.

Suddenly I'm up against the wall in a darkened room. My heartbeat thrums in my ears, in my veins. "What are you doing?" I whisper as the door clicks closed, cutting us off from wondering eyes.

His lips find my neck, answering my question. My hands tighten against his shirt, a soft gasp leaving my lips at the pleasurable sensation. I've never had anyone touch me like this. The way his tongue moves—definitely a player.

"Why are we in here?" I breath out, tilting my head for more. It smells of smoke in here.

"You look innocent, like you don't know what it's like to be touched and kissed and loved. I want to show you."

He's right. I've never had a man this close to me, unless I was stealing something from his pockets.

"Love doesn't come from neck kisses in a dark room." I push my hands against his chest. "We can talk first. I want to know you."

His hands pause on my body. "Who said anything about love?" He says the word with so much loathing. Love. As if it is something that should be wiped from existence.

His lips continue with their job, as he trails kisses up towards my jaw and then to my lips. I've never been kissed. I turn my head. A kiss is a determining factor. If I'm a bad kisser, he will be repulsed. All of this will be ruined. I won't see my mother smile.

"Please, let's slow down."

But he doesn't, his hands continue to roam into more uncomfortable territories. I'm afraid that if I am forward and say no, he will jump to the next girl and forget about me.

Let her go.

CHAPTER 6

Zayen: I just wanted a damn break from the world. A second of silence and darkness. Nawaz took that, too.

Her breath hitches as soon as I light the lantern on the wall beside me. The thief. The liar. The last girl in this place that I should be aiding.

Ali heaves out a sigh and drops his cigarette beside me, most likely thinking the same thing that I am: we are going to get into so much khara for helping this girl.

But it would be much more painful to stand in the dark and watch her give in to something she clearly doesn't want. The way many others have, desperate for the cruel prince's affection.

"Do you do this to all your conquests, prince?" I say the word with as much contempt as I can. This is what leadership looks like these days. "Lead them into a dark room and take advantage of the fact that you have power."

His nostrils flare, and he lets go of her. He steps towards Ali and I as if he is ready to pummel our heads into the wall. "We flirted. I offered to show her more of my tattoos and she accepted. That is more than enough consent for me."

My eyes shift to hers, but she's staring at the floor. What he said before must be true—she doesn't know what it is like to be touched, or kissed. She most definitely does not know how to flirt, but Nawaz will take anything as flirtation.

Ali throws his hands up. "Listen, bro, just leave her alone and we can all just—"

"Don't call me bro. What were you two doing in here? Watching in the darkness, like perverts."

I step on Ali's cigarette, concealing it. Nawaz does not need to know. Although he can probably smell it. "We were ensuring that there are no threats in every corner of the palace. But clearly the only threat here is you."

Insulting him is going to get us nothing, but it sure is satisfying. Almost as satisfying as it would be for him to swing at me, so I can knock him down to the ground.

His silence spurs me on. "Not only a threat to women, but to the entire kingdom. Idiocracy—"

"Don't you dare call your prince an idiot!" Rage fills the veins in his arms, the fissures in his green eyes. His fists clench.

"Anger is weakness. It shows insecurity. Clearly you don't want to be called an idiot because deep down you know you are—"

There. Suddenly he is closer, swinging his ink-coated fist towards me. Does he not know that I'm a royal guard? That I have spent my entire life being trained to kill.

Before he can regain his stability, I swing a foot forward and knock him off his feet. His grunt fills the silence as he lands on his ass.

"Stop," a soft voice calls.

I lean down and grab his collar, ready to make up for every punch his guards were ordered to give me. I finally have a justified reason to.

"Stop! I did flirt with him. He's right." The thief. The liar. The damn gold digger.

There are enough bad people in this world. For some reason, I kept hoping she wasn't one of them; that I gave her that ruby bracelet for a reason.

The door swings open, the loud bang of it making us all pause. "What is going on here?" The stern voice of the Hakeem overpowers every other sound. His eyes reflect the fire in the lanterns.

I wonder what he thinks, seeing me standing over his beloved son. If he will kill more for it. "Come with me. Now." His eyes find the thief. "You too. Yalla." He turns and walks away, expecting us to follow.

Ali grabs the cigarette butt and shoves it into his mouth to hide it. I cringe. The bottom of my shoe was on that. Ali and I trail behind the theif and Nawaz, side-by-side, to make it look like we are escorting them and not being given a hiding.

As we walk past the indoor garden in the main square, Ali spits the cigarette butt out. He straightens his shirt and continues as if nothing happened.

"You could have just held it in your hands. Nobody would have seen it."

His brown eyes drag to mine. They're the same shade as mine. On the training fields, everyone used to say we were brothers. He is more of a brother to me than Nawaz will ever be.

"You could've told me that earlier, man." He cringes and wipes his tongue with his sleeve.

The thief's eyes are filled with wonder as she walks through the palace, taking in the high ceilings and unnecessarily expensive artworks hung on the walls. Maybe she is planning what she might help herself to.

I wouldn't blame her. Some of the vases and smaller artworks may have gone missing because of me. I gave it to those who needed it more. The Hakeem didn't even notice. I almost wish he did, because then I'd know that he actually cared about the things he wastes so much money on.

When we reach the hall that the Hakeem hosts most of his meetings in, he invites all four of us to sit on the plush cushions with him. "Now, Malaika, could you start by telling me your version of what happened?"

Malaika? I bite my lip to avoid laughing, but a small sound escapes my lips. Either the name is a lie or her mother is sorely disappointed.

The Hakeem watches me with a look that would put me six feet under. A look given to those he sends straight into the Aleamiq prison.

"You are being disrespectful in front of royalty." He gestures his palm to the thief.

Royalty? This has to be a damn joke. I knew she was a liar, but to claim to be royalty? What is she getting out of this?

"Pathetic," I mumble under my breath, making sure she hears.

She watches me, her hands clasping together over her crossed legs. "It was my fault," she says to the Hakeem. That must be the closest thing to the truth that has left her lips since she arrived here. "I was flirting with Nawaz and things went a bit too far. Your guards thought I was uncomfortable and tried to help me. Their intentions were good."

"Is this true?" The Hakeem asks the rest of us. Nawaz easily nods, and Ali turns to me for a response.

She was telling him to stop and he wouldn't. Why is she protecting this worthless prince?

Because she still wants his affection—No, she wants his damn money. "You're pathetic," I tell her, lacing my words with venom.

"Zayen!" The Hakeems voice booms loud enough to feel like a slap. I'm sure he wants to hit me.

When I don't respond, his gaze flickers between the thief and I. She seems to be sinking into herself. Silence settles over us like dust in an abandoned home.

"As an apology for being disrespected, I would like to invite you to stay in our home. What do you say?" There's a warmth in his voice, but I've learnt to see what genuine warmth looks like and this is not it.

I want to tell her to run; that if she stays, she'll see a world much worse than anything outside these palace walls. Seeing the poor suffering hurts, but seeing the way the rich behave when there are people dying right outside is something that leaves scars on a soul that can never be healed.

But of course she is going to accept. More time with the prince means that she is more likely to take his riches.

She nods, a smile lighting her features. It lights her face, making her look more innocent. Her eyes crease, almost as if the smile is real. I hate to admit it, but her smile is beautiful. If only it wasn't a lie, like the rest of her façade.

"For disrespecting the royalty of Diyar, I am going to assign you as her guard," the Hakeem tells me. "So that you may it up to her in the coming nights. Is that understood?"

I'm shaking my head before he can finish. "Wh—?"

"Is that understood?" I don't know what threats lie behind his stern voice, but I have been here my entire life and I have seen what this man is capable of.

"Yes."

He nods slowly and then glances over at each of us. "Good. Now, let us go back down and be civil. People are watching. You especially, Nawaz. Do not disappoint me."

"Na'am, papa," Nawaz agrees.

"Don't call me papa. You are not a child." The Hakeem grunts as he gets back to his feet and straightens out his white thobe.

The prince's face falls, his eyes dropping to the ground in shame. The thief seems to sympathise with him, her features softening at his reaction. As if for a moment she is not acting, and truly wishes to reach out and touch him.

I can't find it in me to feel a morsel of sorrow for him. The Hakeem told me to stop calling him papa the day Nawaz was born. I was a child.

CHAPTER 7

Alara: From the moment the Hakeem mentioned my 'royalty', the unnamed guard's eyes have pierced through me over and over—multiple assassinations happening in his head.

It doesn't help that his punishment for helping me is having to guard me. But there's no point worrying about it, because I am trying to win the affection of a prince, not a guard.

But he won't stop following me.

The shuffle of my footsteps is the only sound is the grand hallways of the palace. His footsteps are silent. He must have been trained to go by unheard; unnoticed.

But I can feel him watching me. Every time I take a corner, I see his shadow shifting across the candle light.

I stop at the edge of a turn and press myself back against the smooth walls. The people in the portraits hung along the hallway seem to watch me, holding their breaths with me. The silence starts to make me feel like I have lost my hearing, like I am going crazy and there is nobody following me.

Until he steps around the corner. I jump out of the shadows. "Ah!"

He doesn't blink twice, his face stone cold and staring ahead. The set of his jaw is tightened. "Why did you leave the ma'duba?" he asks.

I walk to stand in front of him, but still, he looks past me and refuses to meet my gaze. "What?" I wave my hand in front of his face, wishing that he would look at me again with that charm that glittered in his eyes before he realised I am not a good person mmm mmm. "You think I'm going to steal something?"

"Yes, and thanks to you, you're my problem now. There's many other things I'd rather do than—"

"Follow me around like a lost puppy?" I roll my eyes. No, I don't blame him for thinking I am going to steal. But he can at least meet my eyes when he speaks to me. He's treating me the same way I've felt every day in the souks. Invisible.

He doesn't react to my words. That's not surprising.

"I'm not going to steal." I try to stand on my toes to get into his line of vision, but I'd need a ladder to get close to his line of sight. "I wanted to get away, okay? Prince Nawaz moved to the next girl so fast."

"What did you expect? Do you think that because you're beautiful you're going to win the heart of a prince?" His voice roughens. Then he notices his words—beautiful—and his eyes fall to mine for a second, his lips parting. But he quickly closes his mouth, knowing that retracting those words would be pointless.

"Just so you know, I'm not here to take anything from the palace or from the prince. I made a dea—" I shut my mouth. Why am I telling him about my deal with the Hakeem? It's not necessary to prove myself to a man who doesn't even want to look me in the eyes. I gently tug at the sleeves of my dress.

His lack of curiosity bothers me. There is not even the raising of an eyebrow at the information I nearly gave away. I want to wrap my hands around his large neck and choke him until he reacts. I'd bet he still wouldn't.

"Fine, if you won't even look at me then just keep following me from a distance." I turn and sprint as fast as my legs can take me. I didn't say I would be easy to follow.

My footsteps thud against the majalis carpets that line the polished stone floors. I can't hear his footsteps, but he is a trained guard and I am not going to slow down to check.

My breath rushes in and out of my lungs at a constant flow until all I can feel is my pulse pumping through every inch of my body.

Finally, six sets of doors come into view. I push through a random one and pull it shut, turning to press myself against the engravings set into the wooden doors. Until I realise that all six doors lead into the same place—a library. A huge library.

I step forward, finally understanding what it feels like to experience wonder. An endless amount of stories waiting to be told; information waiting to be studied. Thoughts and theories and work that was once nothing but a thought, now on papyrus. Rows upon rows, so tall that it needs huge ladders to reach the top shelves.

My fingers brush along the spines of the books, until I reach one with a hardened cover protecting the pages.

One of the doors clicks closed. "Your mom did a really bad job of raising you, if you don't understand the basic concept of not taking what is not yours." His voice makes me turn towards him, his words searing into my chest.

My mom. She gave up her life, her joy, so that I could live. "You don't know anything about me." That urge to choke him returns.

"And I'd like to keep it that way, sariq." Sariq. He is calling me a thief. He isn't wrong.

Keeping my eyes locked on his, I pull the book out of its place on the shelf and tuck it under my arm. Maybe I will keep it, just to piss him off.

"Put it back." His weapons shift as he walks closer to me, watching me like a lion hunting it's prey. Finally, he's looking at me again.

I press it tighter against my body. "What if I don't?"

He unsheathes a small dagger, the handle dusted with different gems. The silver blade is inscribed with words and letters that are hard to read from where I stand.

With each slow step he takes, the silence becomes louder and the space around us feels tighter. When he finally reaches me, the smell of his oud hugs my senses. Just like that day in the market, where he handed me the stolen bracelet and then let me go.

But this time, instead of letting me go, he presses me back into the shelves with the blade of his dagger to my neck.

"You're not going to kill me." I don't flinch away from the blade, even as he presses it harder against my skin.

"Why wouldn't I?" He has a small beauty spot beneath his left eye that softens his otherwise strong features. His hand tightens around his blade, causing the muscles in his arm to shift. "Why wouldn't I?" he repeats, his voice hardening.

"Because you know that of all the things I could have stolen in a palace, a book means nothing. Somewhere inside you, you know I'm not a bad person and that's why you haven't told anyone the truth about me."

His anger seems to grow. Maybe it is frustration because he knows I am right. "A book means nothing? Some of these books hold lifetimes of work and knowledge. Maybe you should stop stealing and start reading."

"I . . ." He likes reading. "I read." I straighten my back.

He tilts my chin up with the fuller of his blade. "What, then? What do you read?" His eyes stare into mine, so deep and assessing that I regret wanting him to look at me at all.

Warmth fills my cheeks without my permission as I think of the romance stories I've read. They're the closest I've gotten to experiencing love. I've never made physical contact with a man either—and I wouldn't say the touch of a blade counts, no matter how close he is.

As if reading my mind, he says, "Romance, huh? I'm not surprised. Don't get excited. Me wishing death upon you is the farthest thing from romance." What does he mean by 'not surprised'?

"I didn't think this was romantic." I want to push him away, but he smells nice.

"Then why is your face so red?" His eyes trail over my cheeks, to my lips, then back up to my eyes.

"What's your name?" I ask, hoping to change the topic fast.

"What's your name?" His head tilts to the side. "I'm certain it's not Malaika."

Am I that easy to read? "You're certain?" I shift back, pushing his knife away with the palm of my hand.

"It would be such a shame if your mother named you 'angel' and you ended up as a lying thief instead. So for the sake of irony, I'm hoping it's not."

"I won't tell you, because I do not want my name to be ruined by your lips." It's a bad idea to admit that Malaika isn't my real name but he has no way to prove it.

The soft curve of his lips tilts upwards into a smirk. "Trust me, my lips can do much more than ruin a name."

That's enough. I need him to get away. If I tell him that, he'll want to get closer to piss me off. So I do the opposite.

Prove it.

CHAPTER 8

Zayen: The nerve of this woman. Kiss me. Why would I ever do such a reckless, unnecessary thing?

My response could have been nicer. I told her the truth, that I'd rather kiss the floor. If she was hurt by my words, by my rejection, she did not show it. In fact, she seemed happy that I stepped away.

I've never seen the point in kissing. Tongues have the most disgusting texture, and then I am expected to pretend to enjoy it?

What I said was the truth. I would much rather lick the floor of a souk than kiss anyone—especially her. It's a pointless expression of love and desire, that ultimately gains us nothing. A thousand kisses or none, this life still ends with death. There's no need for the unnecessary.

The girl I once kissed was beautiful. She was enticing. She had the curves of a goddess and the voice on an angel and yet her tongue was devastatingly human.

I paid a price for that kiss. Nothing will ever convince me to give up my heart for a kiss. Not again. Certainly not for a thief.

The dining hall that held hoards of people, all lining up to raise their status with the Hakeem, is now empty. Except for the girl in the red dress who has sat on the same cushion for over an hour, staring at her hands which are folded up in her lap. Her hair falls forward, soft curls brushing her hollow cheeks. She needs food.

I stop in front of her, and knock my foot against hers. Surprisingly, her shoes are below average, the soles almost peeling off. I didn't notice before.

She looks up, the surprise in her eyes dimming when she realises I am not who she wanted me to be. She brushes her curls away from her face, carefully tucking them behind her ears.

I am not the prince who disappeared upstairs with a girl in a blue shawl. Who would want a knight in shining armour when they could have a prince?

If she has been sitting here the entire time, it means that she watched the cleaning service neaten up the room. She must have put up quite the fight, because the pillow she is sitting on is the only one remaining. The Hakeem will not be happy.

"It's almost sad. You lose a man's attention and suddenly you do not know what to do with yourself." I hold my hand out to help her stand up.

She stands on her own, refusing to touch me, and ends up closer than she expected. Her head tilts up to watch me, her expression filled with irritation, hidden behind a wall of defence. "Shut up."

My chest shakes with unexpected laughter. I'm sure she does have some royal blood in here, distantly. She has the attitude of royalty. Maybe they will get along after all. "Don't tell me to shut up, sariq." I turn and walk to the door. "Regardless, you're going to follow me. Otherwise you can sit in this empty hall for the rest of the night."

The silence that follows is broken after a few seconds, by the sound of her shoes shifting against the floor.

Half of the castle is reserved for rooms. The majority of them are left empty, with the Hakeem and Nawaz on the second floor, and the guards shoved into the basement. The first floor is saved for visitors, which are rare save for women invited by Nawaz to stay the night. He would never let a woman into his room.

The palace was originally built without toilets, because sewage systems hadn't existed yet. People had to keep their waste in buckets.

If that were still the case, Nasir would not handle it well. There would be endless complaints. I know my bucket would go right on top of his head.

There are many options of rooms I could have given the thief, but I am going to give her the smallest room with a window that has no view. She deserves much less.

Stepping aside, I allow her through first. The room is still twice the size of mine. She will probably complain about it and ask for more, since she is in the palace.

Her eyes search the room and then stick to the bed. "This is mine?" she asks, her voice breaking ever so slightly.

"No, none of it is yours. But you will be here for however long the Hakeem let's you stay. Maybe a week. Then you—" I shut my mouth when I notice the shimmer in her eyes in the light of the dim lanterns. Tears.

Her eyes meet mine and she quickly shifts to look away, her head tilting up to the ceiling. I study the side profile of her face—the curve of her lips, the rosiness of her cheeks, her thick eyelashes that line her eyes. A sadness twists each of her features.

As quick as it came, her emotion is gone and she is nodding. Her face hardens to stone, a feat I am impressed she can do. Not many people that I have met can handle their emotions so well. "This will do." Her chin lifts, her gaze defiantly meeting mine.

"You don't have to act around me, sariq. I know what you are."

"Oh really?" She folds her arms across her chest. Her lips press tightly together. "Tell me, then."

As much as I dislike her for coming her, for lying, and for getting me into trouble—which will mean more eyes on me and less possibility of going to see Saad and Aya—I can see why she is here. "Your life is not easy. Things are obviously hard. If you had money, if you had anything, you wouldn't resort to stealing or lying. That's the only reason I haven't said anything. Because life is not easy for everyone; not everyone was born in a palace with a throne awaiting them."

Her expression shifts into something I don't recognise, and for a moment I wish I could tell what thoughts are crossing her mind. I want to know how close I am to the truth.

Instead of denying it, she says, "That's why you gave me the bracelet."

"Of course it was. That's why I asked you what you're going to use it for. Where is your mother now? Did you—?"

Her eyes shift to the door and then back to me. She widens them to indicate someone is behind me, which silences me immediately.

"How do you know who her mother is?"

CHAPTER 9

Alara: The prince is standing at my door. Shirtless. From the way his hair is ruffled, it is clear that he did many things to that girl in the blue shawl.

"Because . . ." Zayen's eyes find mine, panic and uncertainty flashing like flares shooting into the night sky. "Because I wanted to marry her."

What? It takes everything to avoid reacting to that statement; to avoid screaming at the most unbelievably stupid excuse I have ever heard. Clearly he is not great at thinking on his feet.

"What?" the prince asks, echoing my thoughts. What if the prince backs off now, because he thinks that this guard wants me? What if this man just ruined everything? "Zayen, you're in love with this girl?"

Zayen. That's his name. Rough and powerful. It almost suits him.

He refuses to look at me. Good! He should be ashamed, because now the prince is not going to want me anymore. Maybe that was his plan, to let this backfire and then kick me out.

I take a deep breath. Or maybe he saved me from being exposed. Possibly being locked up for treason and left to rot in the underground prison with no windows or oxygen.

Because what would I have said? How would he know anything about my mother? I have a lot of practice being a thief, but not a liar.

But now I have lost.

Nawaz steps up closer to me, most likely ready to escort me out. His hand touches my arm, but his touch is gentle. "Do you feel the same way, Malaika? Do you love him?"

"No," I shake my head rapidly. "And . . . And my mother didn't like him anyways."

"Ouch." A laugh escapes Nawaz's lips, almost sounding like it is exactly what he wanted to hear. "Unrequited and rejected by her mother. I'm not surprised." His eyes seem to turn to slits when his gaze finds Zayen's.

Those words leave an uncomfortable feeling in my stomach. I'm not surprised. Kicking someone who is down is never an attractive quality, no matter how much I want to want the prince.

My stomach growls, breaking the hollowed silence.

They both turn to me. Their burning gazes make me take a step back. I don't like coming off as vulnerable, especially not around two men who I do not know.

Suddenly, Nawaz's smile is back, creating a mask over whatever is hidden behind it.

The other girls must have left. I must be his last option. That must be the only reason why he is here, taking my hand and leading me towards the kitchen.

Zayen trails behind us, until Nawaz turns to him. "Leave."

"No." His jaw tightens. "Your khara got me in this position in the first place." His eyes flicker to mine. "And this clueless girl chooses food over safety. She chooses you over safety. So no, I won't leave."

But Nawaz barely acknowledges that Zayen has said a word as he steps into the kitchen.

This palace keeps leaving me in wonder. Having seen the lush gardens in the middle of the hallways, the wealthy attendees of the ma'duba handing gifts to the Hakeem, the gigantic library with more books than a person could read in two lifetimes—I was expecting the same of the kitchens. Excess. Grandiosity. But instead, the kitchen is small, nearly home-like, and filled with the smell of a mixed of spices.

A man in patterned purple pants and an oversized white shirt stands at the stove, a huge wooden spoon in his hands. My mouth immediately begins to water.

"Afan, is that whole pot for you," Nawaz teases. There's a kindness to his voice that was not there moments ago. Why is he on a teasing basis the chef? Why is his voice laced with hatred when he speaks to Zayen?

"Of course the whole pot is for me. How do you think I got this belly?" He places a hand on his stomach. "Never trust a skinny chef, right? At least that is the excuse I use when it's two in the morning and I'm snacking on samoosas."

Nawaz walks over and places a hand on the man's shoulder, then gestures to me. "I want to treat this beautiful woman. Can you help me?"

My cheeks heat. I've never been called beautiful before. In fact, most times I am barely acknowledged as a woman—beneath my ragged clothes and tied up hair.

The chef's eyes assess me. "Yes, I think I know what you'll like." He scratches his stubbled cheeks and nods, deep in thought. "Yalla, I'll prepare it and have it brought to you."

Brought to me. If this is what royalty feels like, I don't want it. I'd rather learn. That is the way my father raised me when I was young. 'Sharpen your mind and it will become your most powerful weapon", he would always say. "Could you . . . show me?"

He chuckles, interest lifting his brows. "I was only going to pick you some litchis and slice some pear for you."

"Wh—?" I don't know what those are, but if I ask, I might give away that I am not royalty. It may be a food only the upper class know of. "Oh, okay. Then I will be in my room. Thank you."

The less I say, the better. I know that Zayen is not spilling my secret, but from the expression every time I meet his eyes, I know that I am not his favourite person. He will not save me again. I need to be careful.

But I'm used to protecting myself, figuring out new ways to make it to the next day. I've had years of practice.

I'll be fine.

The sweet juice of a litchi bursts in my mouth. My eyes flutter shut. I want litchis every day.

My hands are sticky from the exotic fruit. From the coarse skin covering it, I would have never thought it would be so delicious and sweet inside.

I'm adding it to my 'one day'. One day I will have a home, hidden beneath lush green trees. One day, I will be able to sit in bed and do nothing but read a book. One day, I will step out into my garden and pick litchis to eat.

We all have dreams that we strive for. The life that we are living will never satiate us, whether we have a million gold coins or zero. We will always want more. It's what keeps us living, the desire for more.

Heavy footsteps begin to retreat, indicating that Zayen must be leaving. He must think I am distracted enough by food to not hear the slow shift of wood. But it is exactly what I have been waiting for—an escape.

I need to explore the castle without him, I need to search for answers and clues and anything to know more about the prince. To know more about what softens him and hurts him. That is the only way I will be successful in this game.

I rinse my hands underneath the water bowl and push the wooden door of my bedroom open.

Glancing back at my room once again. This room is something I never thought I would get to see with my own eyes, not even in my dream of one day. That soft cloud for sleeping on . . . I am sure if I had one back home, I'd never leave it. Forget about survival.

I remember from what have read in books and stories about this land, the royalty would sleep on mats and would have the pleasure of a soft pillow for their heads. Now, they have this. Innovation has truly taken us to a new world.

In the darkness of the hallways, I trail my fingers along the walls to guide me. Hushed whispers seem to come from every corner of the palace, like there are many things happening around me that I have no idea about.

When I walked past during the day, all of the rooms on this floor seemed empty. The prince must have a room on a level above mine, which is good because that is most likely where he will be. The further he is from me, the more I can find about him in this place. I could ask, but the truth is not always a commonality with those in power.

The muffled voices become clearer and I halt, holding my breath in the darkness. They're coming from inside the walls.

I keep walking, until my fingers find the slightest incline against the wall. A strange sensation twists my gut, telling me that I am about to find out more than I had bargained for; that I should turn around and go to sleep.

The door is just like the one that the prince snuck me into, when he was trying to make a move. It's moulded into the walls, unnoticeable.

I dig my nails into the space where the wall and the door separate, tugging until my fingers start to ache. This door must not be used often.

Finally, the smallest slant of light shines through the gap. I press my face closer, the view becoming clearer.

"Take her."

CHAPTER 10

Alara: I couldn't drag my eyes away.

I wanted to—I swear, I wanted to. As they shoved the woman onto a empty metal table, her mouth muzzled like an animal unable to do anything but glare with ferocious eyes. Her dark hair pools around her as they tie her down and rip open her clothes.

One of the guards that I have never seen before sorts through an assortment of items made to cut and deform human skin. He lifts one up to assess it. It's a pair of scissors, the tips razor sharp and easily able to cut into human skin.

He places it back down on the tray beside the table. The woman watching, sighs in relief and learns her head back, until he picks up a strange object that seems to be shaped like a spice pestle, but the surface of it is covered in dull spikes. As if someone had hammered old needles into the surface. The guard seems to be satisfied with that one, and hands it over to another guard.

That is when the Hakeem speaks, as the woman eyes the weapon of choice. "We have given you more than enough time to make your choice. What shall it be?"

She stays silent, her chin tilting up to defy him. If she could open her mouth, I'm sure she would spit at the floor where he stands.

"Very well." He nods, and the guards take action.

Not even the muzzle could stop the screams that left her.

And still, my feet don't move. But my hands shake, uncontrollably. Why? There is not a thing that this woman could have done to deserve something like this.

The Hakeem is right there, watching like a curious student searching for answers. "Anything you have to add, now?" His voice is cold, matching the expression on his face. So different to the smile that he carried earlier.

She can barely catch her breath. Pained sobs rattle her body. The blood drips down her body, soaking her torn clothes and the table beneath her.

A hand weaves around my mouth and pulls me back, silently shutting the door. No. No. No. I know I should fight, but my brain refuses to co-operate, probably because it is stuck on the image of that poor woman.

The feeling of bone deep fear makes it impossible to scream. The same feeling as jumping from a high building—a fear so paralysing that I forgot to scream, I forget to blink, I forget to breathe.

The cold fingers holding my lips shut finally let go. I turn, pushing against a hard chest, to find the prince. He is assessing me warily. His golden brown hair falls is ruffled as if he had just woken up. He slowly grips onto my wrists, stopping me from pushing him away.

Each breath feels too slow, taking an eternity to fill my lungs. Finally, I regain the ability to speak. "Look, I know I wasn't that nice to you but please don't do this. I—please. Please don't do that to me. I won't say anything. My m—" My mom. If I die, what happens to her? At some point our neighbour will get tired of babysitting and leave her. "Please."

He tilts his head to the side, not saying a word. His eyes are darkened in the empty hallways. There are no guards around. I may not be able to fight a prince, but I could run from one.

So I do.

I turn on my heels and go as far as I can, avoiding the wooden tables that sit at spaced intervals holding candles or vases. The carpet makes it easier to run through the halls.

I can see it so much clearer now, the small indents in the walls that were previously unnoticeable. Now they are all that I can see. So many hidden doors, so many secrets.

That woman's scream continues in my mind, unending.

Until the prince catches up to me, grabbing me. His grip jerks us to a stop, causing him to crash into me. It takes us both down to the ground, and he rolls on top of me, pinning me to the rugs and stopping me from running again. "You really thought you could run from me?"

He isn't putting all of his weight on me, but I can still feel the hardness of his body, the heat radiating from him. I hope he can't see my double chin at this angle.

I tilt my chin up, shame refusing to let me meet his eyes. I barely made it down the hall. I've always been able to outrun people. I would have been a terrible thief without that skill.

"Get off." My chest rises and falls rapidly as I try to catch my breath. I don't care about the deal. I don't care about him liking me. I don't care about the money. When life is on the line, everything else ceases to matter. It's a funny thing, how priorities can change in an instant.

"Don't forget who you're talking to." His eyes slip to my lips. He likes it when I disrespect him? Men are strange.

"Does . . . Are you going to kill me?" Is that a question you should ask a killer? Wouldn't they say no, even if they were going to?

He seems like someone that would break a heart, but not stop it from beating all together. Then again, people in power do what they have to in order to remain in power.

But it wouldn't make sense to kill me.

It suddenly becomes glaringly obvious, the position we are in and how empty it is here. He could do much worse than kill me.

I place my hand on his chest. His shirt is the softest silk I have ever felt. One of these must cost more than everything I own combined.

"Possibly, if you keep talking to me as if I am a peasant." He glances down at my hand, then meets my eyes again. "What are your intentions here, Malaika?" The way he says that name is melodic. It confuses me.

"To survive," I say truthfully.

"Nothing more than survival?" he asks, his expression is saying a million things that his lips are not.

"What more is there? We work to survive; marry to survive; we eat to survive. We live every day hoping to make it to the next, and hoping that the people we care for do too."

He opens his mouth to say something, then decides against it.

"What?" I ask.

"That's . . . not the way royals think." My eyes widen, realising my mistake too late. He notices my shift of expression and stands, holding his hand out to help me up. "Plus, it sounds unbelievably boring spending your life trying not to die."

Easy to say when you live in a palace.

I take his hand, and he easily lifts me. My eyes trail to another door in the wall that is now closed, the screams of the woman no longer audible. Silence seems to vibrate around us. I want to ask why they're doing that to her, but questions can be danger-ous—and I have already spoken too much.

He must know what is happening inside these walls. He didn't look shocked, or worried. "Ask what it is you want to ask," he says, exasperated.

But there's so many questions swarming in my head. "Will she be okay?"

He glances at the secret door. His back straightens and he rubs a hand against the back of his neck. His Adam's apple bobs. "We'll see."

We'll see? How could he be this calm? I take a step back. "What do they want? Did you know her? Did she stay here?" Am I next?

"I don't know. No. And no." He steps closer, reaching out to take ahold of my wrist, but I step out of reach. My hands fold against my chest. I don't trust him. He has his fathers smile; the one that hides too much.

"You're the prince. Stop them." I can feel my chest caving in on itself.

The previous plan doesn't matter anymore. There is no way to guarantee that the Hakeem didn't invite me to stay, so that he could do the same thing to me. I have to leave—but I can't let the prince know that.

He smiles. This fool smiles. I have never been a violent person, but that smile makes me want to hit him.

But looking a bit closer, it's not a smile of satisfaction or happiness. A small, forced tilt of the lips. It's an empty smile. "Do you really think my father would listen to my command?" he asks, as if the idea of it is ridiculous. "He is the Hakeem. He does as he pleases."

"No, I can't allow it." I step towards the door, but he blocks me.

I tilt my head up to glare at him, ending up closer than I would have liked. His silk shirt shifts, reflecting the soft light of the moon. "Now is not the time to be a hero. It will cost y—"

He is wrong. Because it will not cost me. If I can save one person—one life, then I will die successful.

I throw the secret door open, and every eye turns to me.

Run.

Chapter 11

Alara: The girl screams to me—telling me to run, but it is muffled by the muzzle. She squirms in their grip, but it's too late.

There is no way to un-see this, and from the way the Hakeem has his jaw set and his gaze unblinking, he knows it too.

Maybe I should have brought a weapon. Maybe I should have thought this through.

The door slams closed and the prince takes my face, making me look at him in the darkness of the room. "That was really stupid. You have to go. Now."

But the door slams open and two guards grab me by my arms. Their grips are painfully strong, their fingers digging into me so hard it starts to ache. They shove me to my knees.

I try to pull back, away from them, but it's too late. From the way Nawaz's face has fallen, he knows it too. My eyes try to find his, to ask him the silent question—what are they going to do to me? But he refuses to meet my gaze. That says enough.

"What are you doing outside of your quarters?" The Hakeem asks. He steps in front of my kneeling form, looking down at me from the tip of his nose. "The least you could do as a guest in my home is mind your business, girl."

He says the word girl, as if it is intended as an insult.

I say nothing, because there is nothing that needs to be said. If I ask more questions, I will only make things worse.

He sighs. "Where is your guard?" The question is resigned, filled with disappointment, as if he doesn't want to do whatever he is about to do.

"I snuck off when his back was turned," I lie. Zayen has had my back while I was here. The least I could do is not get him in trouble for whatever it is he is doing at night. "I just wanted to walk around, maybe find another garden."

"And you thought that there would be a garden behind this door?" He gestures to the secret door, that is most definitely not leading to a garden.

"No, I just heard screams and I thought someone might need help."

"You're a royal, not a superhero." I am neither. But what use is it to be alive, to survive, if I can't help others when it is needed? "Put her in Aleamiq."

No.

I've heard stories of Aleamiq before—all of them horrible. All of them based on myth. The meaning of the name is 'the deep'. People say that it is named to represent the bottom of the ocean, a place where the darkness is so haunting that people see more than they wish; where the pressure is so intense that it can crush bones.

They drag me back up to my feet, and I try to push backwards, to get out of their grasp. I turn my head back to Nawaz, silently pleading with him to help, even when I know he won't.

He won't defy his father. He doesn't have any reason to protect me, a stranger. Plus, there is no guarantee that a man like the Hakeem would not put his own son down in the prison.

The walk down to the prison feels endless, each step seems to go in slow motion. My body feels as if it has been filled with lead. The sound of the guards shoes against the floors echoes in my ear, like the beating of drums before an execution.

That's what this is. An execution. I am never going to get out, never going to escape whatever it is that is waiting for me.

I am never going to see my mother.

When she kneels down on my sleeping mat and wonders where I have gone. When my neighbour walks out on her, re-alising that I am not coming back. When she stops eating, stops caring. Stops breathing.

Because of me.

I am lead down a steep set of stairs, taken underground. There are crackling fires lit against the walls between each door. It seems to be the guards quarters. Zayen might be somewhere down here.

The sounds of people groaning in empty, helpless despera-tion, comes from somewhere further down the passage. Each step forward makes the sound clearer, until it's all I can hear. It's in every breath, every blink, every move. The sound of pain.

Another set of guards wait at the entrance of what must be the prison. It is sealed with a humongous wooden door that does nothing to block the smell of death and rot.

It is exactly as the stories make it seem. People who have lost their minds. Darkness that makes one see things that aren't there. A cold that seeps into bone marrow and does not leave.

A recreation of hell.

Large hands wrap around the bars of the cell. "What the—?"

Before he can get more than a word out, I jump to my feet and rush up to him. The cold down here has numbed my body. "Zayen, did you know?"

"What are you doing in here? I wasn't even gone for an hour? All you had to do was not leave your room." I can barely see him, except for a slight outline in the darkness.

"Do you know?" I ask again. I need more information. "Inside the walls. The people. What they're doing." That woman. The muzzle. The screaming.

His eyebrows crease. "Did they lock you up for reasons of insanity?"

"No, you're not listening to me." I lean my head against the cold bars, slowing my breathing. "I found a door in the wall, like the one that you were smoking in." He tried to hide it, but I saw. "There was a woman that was crying for help and the Hakeem was there. They were torturing here. Why? What do you know?"

He steps back. His head turns as he checks to make sure there is nobody in the hallways, before stepping close again.

The smell of his cologne surrounds me, giving me an escape from the horrid smells in this place. "Which door? What else did you see?"

"Nothing, but Nawaz knows. He tried to get me out of there but I couldn't leave that woman. You need to find her. You need to help her."

"Why are you so worried about saving a woman you don't know?" he asks.

I glance back up at him, his face is covered in shadows. "Because that could be me. I would like to believe someone would have the decency to help me if they saw . . . that happening to me." The device, that looked like it was made in a rush with a a few pins and some wood, being dragged against her skin.

In the silence between us, the wails of people in the cages around me seem to reverberate in my ears. The sounds of their pain and suffering so clear that it makes me wish I could hear nothing at all.

"Listen, I'm going to get you out." His voice is calm, pensive. The rough, deep sound of his accent is yet another escape in this place. It makes me wish he could stay. "You saw more than I did. What do you think I should do?"

It's a long shot, but . . . "Nawaz." He was the only one who has a morsel of concern on his face as I was being dragged off by the guards and left to rot down here. He is the only one that that has a chance of getting through to the Hakeem. "Talk to him. Try to reason with the Hakeem. Convince him that I won't say a word."

"Nawaz." His voice lowers, his hands dropping to his sides to form fists. "That's the only option?" He seems to be detaching from the thought, from the idea of helping me.

"You don't have to . . ." I know he hasn't been particularly fond of me. If he did absolutely nothing, it would be understandable. I am nothing but, as he calls me, a sariq.

He huffs, seemingly frustrated that I told him he doesn't have to. "I'll talk to him."

My heart picks up it's pace, leaving my lungs filled with the old, murky air down here. He doesn't have to do this. But I am grateful that he is. "Why are you helping me?"

He raises an eyebrow, surprised by the doubt in my question. "Because I would like to believe someone would have the decency to help me if they saw me rotting in a dark cage." I open my mouth to say something, but he continues. "And what use is my position as a guard, or even as a relatively decent human, if I can't help those who need it?"

A sigh comes from behind me—barely a whisper of air—followed by a muffled voice. I can help you.

CHAPTER 12

Zayen: A woman steps out of the shadows behind the thief, barely visible in the darkness. She has a strange muzzle on her face which muffled her words. For some reason, I want to be in this cage, stepping in between the two of them.

This thief keeps getting herself into deeper trouble.

Anyone who is willing to make a deal in this place is never willing to trade fairly. They will always ask for too much.

"You. It's you." The thief steps closer, and I immediately want to reach through the bars and pull her back. How could she possibly know this muzzled woman?

"Who are you?" I deepen my voice, hoping to come off as intimidating. She can't clearly see my guard clothing, or the weapons at my side, so my tone will have to suffice. "How can you help, when you are in the same situation as her?"

The woman, frustrated, tries to pull the muzzle from her face but it does nothing. The only reason I can see any movement of hers is because part of our training is fighting in the dark.

I sigh. "Come to the bars. I will cut it for you."

Either this woman has a foolish amount of trust, or she does not care for her life, because she steps closer to me and allows me to lift a weapon to her face.

"Do you think this is a clever position to get yourself into with a stranger?" I ask, even as I lower my weapon.

The muzzle clatters against the floor. When she finally speaks, her voice is gentle and melodic. "You do not need to question my intelligence. I know what battles I can win. The fact that you are down here says that you value something that I have access to." She turns to look behind her.

Is she talking about the thief? "You think I value her? I'll hand you my blade and you can cut her throat, if you wish. Watch if I flinch."

The woman assesses me for a while. "Hmm. So what you said, about wanting to help her, it was a lie?"

"No, I will help her. That does not mean I like her, nor does it mean I will bargain with a stranger for a girl I do not know. So if you were to threaten her life, it would make little difference to me." That is the truth. I don't like liars. I don't like thieves. She is both.

The thief steps forward. Her voice sounds forced, unsure. "What's your name?" She puts a hand on the woman's shoulder. "Is your stomach alright? I saw—" Her breath shudders. "I don't know what I saw. Why would they . . . ?"

"My name is Akilah." The woman lifts a hand to her stomach, where the wound must be. "You ask why they would harm me. The answer is simple. Human beings are selfish, designed to always want more, especially the ones in power.

"Where are you from?" The thief asks. "What do they want that badly? They had a tray of weapons to hurt you. Have you been here—?"

It's moments like this that the thief shows she is no royal. She does not have a way with words. "How will you help?" I ask, instead.

I can't see the thief's expression clearly, but I'm sure she is glaring at me for interrupting her. It doesn't matter, because I don't have a lot of time down here. Another guard could come down here at any time.

Akilah, tortured and captured, still stands tall. "I am from Aleamiq. The real Aleamiq. The Hakeem wants something from my home—a stone that will grant him what he desires most. He could only offer me materialistic things, money or gold or pretty dresses. All things that mean nothing."

The thief scoffs under her breath. It must be hard to swallow those words, when she has grown up with very little. Money only means little to those who have an abundance of it.

"But you saved my life. I owe you a debt," she tells the thief.

"You don't owe me anything."

"You walked in to help me, even though you knew it would cost you. Doing a good deed for others is not a small thing. I want to help."

She lets out a huff of air, then nods. "How will you help? You're locked up in here too. You can't give the stone to the Hakeem. He doesn't deserve that power."

"I can make a deal, that I will bring the stone to the rightful heir of the throne." Even though the woman is not looking at me,

I can feel the suggestion of her words. But there is no way she could know. It is a secret, kept only between me and my father.

"To Nawaz? He could be worse than his father."

"It is a risk we have to take." The woman steps up to the bars, looking for me. "Tell the Hakeem that I request his presence immediately."

The woman, Akilah, sits at the low table in the Hakeem's meeting room. At the Hakeem's side is Nawaz, whose eyes keep drifting to the shivering thief.

She may no longer have the intention to trick the prince into loving her, but it seems like he might have already fallen into the trap. But perhaps love is too strong a word. It only seems that he wants to keep her warm, and then undress her.

It's the same thing he wants for most women he lays eyes on.

I stand at the door, alongside three other guards of the palace. The people who work inside the palace do not become friends, usually. It is dangerous to care, because workers come and go here—and sometimes they go, and are never seen again.

But the guards stay. Guards are trained from teenage years, like Ali and I were, and they swear themselves to the service of the palace. They do not leave, not without a command to do so. I hated every second of swearing to serve my father, when he looked at me like I was nothing.

Now he barely looks at me at all.

"You are agreeing to bring the stone here, to the palace? What has changed your mind?" the Hakeem asks, shifting on the pillow he is sitting on.

"I only swear to deliver it to the heir of the throne." Akilah gestures to Nawaz. "But it is not something I can do alone, so

I'm return for your help. I request the assistance of Malaika and two of your best guards."

The Hakeem doesn't like requests or favours. He regards her in silence. "Very well," he says after some consideration. "You may go on this journey, and I will provide with one guard—however, I will also be sending my son to accompany you, and to ensure you follow through on your word."

Nawaz turns to his father in shock, but says nothing. "Where is the stone?" he asks after recollecting himself.

"We will head towards Diyar, but the location of the stone will be further west." Akilah does not explain more than that. Nawaz clearly has more questions, because there is nothing further west than Diyar, but he says nothing.

Ever the obedient prince.

My fists tighten, remembering every time he sent his guards to my rooms. To do the things he was too cowardly to do himself.

"Very well. We shall set out this evening, if you will allow it." Akilah dips her head, showing her respect.

The Hakeem waves his hand to me. "You will go with them, and protect them. With your life, if you must."

Nawaz meets my gaze, a surprised yet satisfied expression on his face. Once we leave, nothing is going to protect you. I try to send the message through the intensity of my gaze.

"To ensure that both my son and the stone are returned to me, I have created an incentive." The Hakeem gestures with two fingers to the guards standing in the arches behind me.

They bring out three figures, bound and silenced with cloths wrapped around their mouths.

When Aya sees me in the room, she starts crying and tries to reach out for me but one of the guards hold her back. This is not possible.

A soft cry leaves the thief's lips as she rushes to the tallest of the three figures. An older, slim woman with the same brown curls and lack of height as the thief.

Gossamer curtains hanging in front of the arched windows continue to flutter, blowing in wind that suddenly seems to dry and warm. It makes it hard to breath, as if with every breath, desert sand fills my lungs.

The only sound is the soft whisper of the thief speaking to her mother, holding her close.

"Do not worry yourselves. They will have grand rooms and will be fed well. They will not have to lift a finger. I will insure they are cared for," the Hakeem reassures. I wait for the other half of his statement, because there is always a—"However, if within a month, your journey is unsuccessful, their throats will be cut."

At that statement, Saad shifts, trying to get away from the guard and to me. "Ba," he calls for me, then looks towards his sister, tears filling his eyes.

I clench my jaw and look ahead, refusing to meet their eyes; refusing to show that I care. If I do, it will put them in worse danger. I tuck my pain deep down in my chest, and refuse to let it show the way the thief is.

No matter how badly I want to hold them, to whisper against the tops of their heads that they will be okay. That would be an empty promise, when the Hakeem may as well be holding a knife to their necks at this moment.

The thief comes to me, holding onto my forearm. "Do something."

I want to shout at her, to stop being stupid. Does she not see there is a strategy at play, and the Hakeem will exploit our every move? "Go back to your seat," I demand, moving her wrist and pushing her away from me.

I accidentally use too much force, and she stumbles backwards. The look in her eyes nearly makes me apologise, until I see Saad and Aya in their shackles.

This is her fault. If she hadn't come to the palace, stuck her nose into other people's business, none of this would be happening. These innocent children would be safe.

"Sit," I demand, glaring at her. I make sure to make the command sound like I am speaking to a badly behaved dog.

She lowers herself beside Akilah at the table, but her eyes do not leave her mother. The Hakeem dismisses us after confirming that we will be leaving tonight.

"I'm sorry, mama. I love you," the thief calls as her mother is dragged away.

"Alara, be careful," is all her mother says, her voice raspy. So that's her name.

I dare to look at Saad and Aya one last time, unknowing if I'll see them again. They watch me, searching for answers. I wish I could tell them I love them, and that they did nothing wrong.

The anger in my chest causes a ringing in my ears. It makes it impossible to think.

The room empties out, but I don't move. Not until the thief's hands are pushing against my chest. Her eyes are filled with uncontained fury. "How dare you?"

Her fist swings towards my jaw, but I grab it and spin her around, pulling her back against me. I wrap on forearm against the curve of her neck and the other around her midsection to stop her arms from moving.

She tries to shift, but nothing works. She will get out when I allow it. "Stop trying to fight me. I am a trained. royal guard," I say, my voice low.

She squirms against me, but finally stills when she realises it is getting her nowhere. Her breathing is ragged.

I tug my forearm against her throat, pulling her closer to me. Anger pumps through my blood. She deserves to feel this way, because it is her fault. "I hate you, Malaika. I'm going to make sure you wish you had never stepped foot inside the palace."

She huffs. "Good. Because I hate you, too. Now get your hands off me."

CHAPTER 13

A lara: My heart is filled with an ache that feels like it is slowly draining me.

I should have never gotten myself involved with royalty. Even if the situation hadn't ended up as insane as it is, lying to the most powerful man in power could have endangered my mother.

My fist tightens around the small bag hanging from strings at my back. I should have known.

If the Hakeem is honest, then my mother will be safer here for the time being. As long as we get back in time. But I don't like her life being based on a conditional.

Life doesn't work on wishes or hopes, so I will do exactly what the Hakeem wants and make sure we are back in time.

I know it is easier said than done when I do not know what I am walking into.

"Yalla!" Akilah calls out to me from the entrance to the palace.

I walk around the indoor garden that I had previously gawked over, feeling a lack of admiration. Nothing so beautiful should exist in a place like this.

Each step feels filled with lead, until I reach Akilah and step out into the cold evening breeze. It brushes my hair back and I take a deep breath. The first I have taken since seeing my mother tied and being dragged by the hands of a guard.

Akilah is in the same clothing as me—a woven brown coat that feels uncomfortable, like the rough and grainy material of a potato sack. It contrasts the darker brown of her skin, and the scars that are revealed on her arms. This may not be the first time she has been tortured.

Both Zayen and Nawaz are waiting outside already, strapped with an assortment of weapons. They look every bit the warriors that they have been forced to be.

The differences in their status is evident in the small details. The fine stitching of Nawaz's deep blue shalwar kameez, lined with silver thread, compared to Zayen's sirwal and plain cloth shirt; the styling of Nawaz's hair, compared to Zayen, whose hair is shorter and disheveled.

There is a piece of his hair that has curled against his forehead, and it makes me want to brush it back into place. But I will not, because he hates me.

I don't like the way he looks at me, like he want to bury me alive. This situation is not my fault.

There are a group of guards standing outside in a structured line. At first, I think it is to make sure that we leave, but the expressions on their faces say otherwise. Admiration, directed towards Nawaz.

As I ascend the steps, I come to stand in front of Zayen. "Who are those kids?" I ask, tilting my head up to watch him. He didn't even go to say goodbye to them.

I barely got time to hug my mother goodbye. She isn't the same. Of course she wouldn't be, because she was unwillingly removed from her home. She just kept telling me the same thing. You're going home now.

He doesn't bother responding, turning his back to me in ignorance. His posture is rigid, as if he is holding back from saying or doing something.

He probably wants to choke me, or put a weapon to my throat the way he did in the library. Well, I want to do the same to him. He can't completely ignore me for the entirety of the journey.

I don't know what to do. I have never had to deal with a man's anger before. It has always been me and my mother.

Maybe the best way to go about this is to react gently. I place my hand against the muscles of his back, causing them to tense further. "Zayen, I know you blame me for this. I'm sorry." I'll get it out the way, to let there be peace between us. The the only way we're going to succeed with getting what we need, is if we're a team.

He turns. The expression on his face, the rage in his eyes, has not dulled at all. "You're not sorry, sariq, but you will be."

Did he just threaten and insult me? "I am." I reach out to touch him again, hoping that the touch will calm him, but he takes a hold of my wrist to stop me. "I am telling you I am sorry. Why won't you accept it?"

His grip on me tightens. It tugs me closer. I nearly stumble on the tan stone floor. His voice low and threatening, he says, "Because sorry doesn't change anything. Sorry doesn't protect those kids. Your apologies are worthless."

My eyes go to Nawaz and Akilah, who are both watching us. I pull back, feeling like he slapped me. "Why are you—?"

"Stop talking," he demands. "Just stop talking."

A feeling bubbles in my chest that makes me want to shove him to the hard ground. How dare he talk to me like that? Like I'm nothing?

I told him that I hate him, after the meeting with the Hakeem, but it wasn't true. It wasn't true, because I'd like to believe I don't harbour feelings of hate. Now, the words are starting to hold more truth.

"What, are you going to cry?" He barely looks at me. His eyes are already scanning the dark horizon, deciding on our direction.

But I won't give him that power. I won't let him lead, or decide for me. So I push past him and head towards the direction of the mountain, that I know will be a shortcut into Wadi.

I don't cry.

Alara: 1 – Zayen: 0

I cross my arms, a satisfied smile on my lips as we reach the cave of the mountain. Zayen looks surprised, and confused. "How did you know about this place?"

"I always used it when I came to . . ." Steal. "Visit Qadura."

Zayen raises his eyebrow. Don't lie, his expression says, without him saying a word.

I glare. Shut up.

He smirks. I didn't say anything.

Somehow his half-smile manages to irritate me more than when he was being rude directly to my face. Now I simply want him to trip off the edge of the mountain.

Nawaz squints at the roof of the cave. "What does that say?" He pulls the sword that was strapped across his back and pushes the moss and vines out the way. "I don't understand."

It's in Arabic lettering, but it's not words that make sense. It's not anything that we could decipher.

Akilah walks forward. "We don't have time for this. Let's go, unless you want your ruler to make true on his promises to your family." Our ruler? Is she not ruled by the Hakeem?

We continue through the passage until darkness surrounds us, and the only thing we can hear is the shuffle of our shoes against the rocky ground.

When we reach the other side, I look over the view of my home. It's different at night. The air is not as hot, but the usual strange, sour smells float through the air. Many of the houses are dark, not lit up with lamps like they would be in the other towns.

I'm not sure if my mother left something in the house for me to find. You're going home now. I don't know what that means. Maybe she needs me to go home, to find something that might help. It was too cryptic, and she wouldn't say more.

We find our way down the rocky mountain. It is clear, from the way Nawaz occasionally loses his balance, that he is not used to having to be sly footed. He has probably never needed to do anything he didn't want to.

"So, Akilah, could you be more specific with where the stone is? You said west of Diyar, but there is nothing west of Diyar. There's only the ocean."

Akilah looks back at him, glowering like a lioness that wants to devour a mouse. Not because it will be a satisfying meal, but because it wants the mouse to die a gruesome death. "Exactly."

She must dislike him for not standing up to his father. For all the torturing she went through that he knew about.

Wait, did she say exactly? I come to walk beside her as we make our way through the dirt paths between houses. "We're going into the ocean? How are we going to do that?"

"A boat," she clarifies. "Obviously."

That shuts us all up, even Nawaz. Her tone is enough to tell us she does not want to speak to us or answer any questions.

The streets are mostly empty, and I keep my eyes down on my shoes. One foot in front of another, because I do not know how many steps I will need to take but all I need to focus on is the next one.

In the silence, I try to brainstorm how I am going to tell them that I need to go home. There is no good reason, other than the random, unspecific sentence that my mama kept repeating. My mama, who has been so stuck in her own mind that she has barely spoken two words to me in the past year.

It must be important if it was all she would say to me, over and over.

My eyes lift from the dry, sandy ground when I hear the sound of people speaking. There is the gently melody of a woman singing somewhere far away. We somehow reached one of the souks here in Wadi.

Here in Wadi, we can't afford fancy things, but we still use what we have. The items being sold here are vastly different, compared to any of the surrounding towns. Instead of crispy samoosas or sweet kanafa, there are roasted nuts and dates. Instead of silver watches and jewelled sandals there are thin sleeping mats and cracked pottery.

It's different; it's home.

The expressions on my three companions faces are not what I had expected. Nawaz looks curious, having never been to this side of the mountain. Even when I would sneak into the port market, the Hakeem would be there but not the prince. He was most likely busy courting women.

Zayen looks sad, like being here is affecting him in a way that I don't understand. Maybe it's related to those kids, or his past which I know nothing about. It makes me wonder who those kids are, and what his childhood was like.

Akilah, however, looks like she wants to avoid these people and sprint all the way to Diyar to avoid wasting time. Maybe she doesn't like being around people.

There is a soft cry beside me. In Zayen's hand is the wrist of a child whose eyes are filled with horror. His eyes shine with tears in the dim light of the torches set along the walls. "I'm sorry, my mama. She needs help. I thought—"

"What's going on?" Akilah asks, irritated.

In this moment, Zayen looks like a bear grasping onto a baby deer. The boys broken cries are the only thing that pierce the hushed silence. "M-Mama asked me to bring her bread. She's sick. I don't have money."

"He . . ." Zayen seems hesitant to answer. "He was trying to steal my dagger." Sheathed to Zayen's thigh is the same dagger he held to my throat. The handle is bedazzled with an incredible array of jewels.

All I can see is this child sitting at his mother's bed side, promising to bring her something to eat. I wonder if she calls him her 'quwwa'—her strength, the same way my mama used to.

"He should be punished for stealing." Akilah steps towards the child.

No! Forgive me!

CHAPTER 14

Zayen: The skin of the child is as dry as leather, like he has not had enough water. It tugs at my heart.

He tries to pull out of my grasp, begging for forgiveness. "Please, don't hurt me." I won't hurt him. I can't.

I've put enough children in danger. When this child speaks, he sounds scared and alone. It is the same fear that was in Saad's voice when I wouldn't—couldn't—look at him inside the palace.

At this point, people turn to see what is going on. There are hushed whispers about the prince being here. We tried to dress down, to avoid notice, but with a child crying there are many people turning to us.

"We need to go. We'll decide what to do to him later." Akilah grabs the boy, lifts him over her shoulder and turns off into a quieter street.

I glance at Alara. She is already watching me. The way she looks irritates me. I wish she was a man, so I could shove my shoulder into hers. Instead I walk off, down the dark passage where Akilah took the boy.

I follow his whimpering cries until I find him. His body is shaking, his hand pinned against the wall as Akilah threatens to cut off his fingers. "Do you understand the danger of stealing? Never take what does not belong to you. If your mother needs food or treatment, you work until you can afford to buy it for her. Understand?"

"Yes, I understand." He shakes his head rapidly, his eyes darting to me and then behind me.

"I don't think you do. I think—"

"What are you doing with my brother?" An angry voice comes from behind me.

I turn to the direction of the voice. A man, about my height, glares at Akilah. There are four other men behind him, two of them hold onto figures.

The thief and the prince. The two people I was supposed to protect, but didn't. They have black bags placed over their heads. If they're harmed at all, Saad and Aya will be in serious danger.

But they outnumber us, and they have the advantage of two hostages. This is not a good situation for fighting or negotiation.

There is still a fire lighting Akilah's gaze, almost as if she is looking forward to being able to beat the life out of someone.

I assume she is going to let the boy go, but she doesn't. She pulls him closer and twists his neck to the side slowly. "You're going to let them go, or I am going to keep twisting his neck until it pops right off."

At that statement, the boy starts squirming and crying, which makes me regret ever grabbing his hand. I should have let him go and told him to run. The way I did with Alara on the day we met.

"Why would I let them go, when I can kill them just as easily?" He clicks his fingers and the two men holding onto the thief and the prince bring sharp, pointed daggers to their necks. "Draw blood."

The men listen to the command and press the daggers deeper, until blood is dripping from their necks.

"Unfortunately, I believe you care about this child more than I care about those people you have in your hold." Akilah pulls the child's arm back and tugs it so that it dislocates from the socket. He cries out for his brother, legs beginning to wobble. "So let them go, and I will release your brother."

I lower my gaze to the ground. My training as a guard has prepared me for this. We were taught to not be merciful; taught to behave exactly as Akilah is behaving right now, but how can she not care for that child?

His arm is visibly handing out of its socket. Tears and snot run down his face. Fear is clouding his vision as he sobs and calls for his brother, who he calls Rayan.

Rayan grabs a lit torch from the wall, and suddenly the street—the world—becomes darker. The flames of the fire dance in his eyes as he turns and holds it dangerously close to the bag hanging over Nawaz's head. "Do you think I do not realise how invaluable the life of a royal is?"

I step closer to Rayan. Small rocks shift under my boots, making him swing to me, holding the torch out like a fire-tipped sword.

"Your brother was caught trying to steal. We will not hurt him or punish him any further. He has learnt his lesson." I turn and narrow my eyes at Akilah. Her loved ones lives may not be on the line, but mine are. Those kids. "I will send a medic to your house, paid for by the royal family, to treat your brother's arm and your mother's illness."

I will stay true to my word. The Hakeem gave us a good sum of money for this journey.

"That doesn't sound bad—" Rayan lifts his free hand to silence his friend. He walks up to the thief, Alara is what her mother called her, and pulls the bag off of her head.

She doesn't squirm or try to fight. Her eyes narrow and she spits at his face.

He wipes it off and smirks back at me, putting the torch back against the wall. "She's a fighter. I like fighters. Especially beautiful ones." I'm waiting for him to reach his point. "Is she your girl?"

He wants her for himself. The way he looks at her, though, tells me that he will still be generous enough to share her with his friends.

I have to think logically here. If I say no, then he will assume she isn't worth much to me and try to negotiate to keep her. If I say yes, it means he has more power than he should and will ask for more than I might be able to give.

The Hakeem only cares about his son. If Alara doesn't make it back, I doubt he'll blink an eye.

But the more people we have, the easier it might make getting this forsaken stone. She needs to live, to get the stone back to the Hakeem. Because if there's one thing that my father loves more than his perfect little prince, it's power. If that rock doesn't make it to him, I'll lose everything.

"Yes, she's mine."

The thief looks shocked by my choice, as if she was expecting me to send her off with these men.

I wonder what she would say if she knew how strongly I considered it. That if she was not needed, I'd tell them to do whatever they want to her. Thieves and liars get what they deserve, after all.

"Throw in that knife of yours." Rayan nods his chin towards my dagger. The same one his little brother tried to steal from me.

My mother gave it to me, when she thought I would be the next ruler. Before Nawaz was born and everything changed. I will not trade for it.

"No. Pick something else."

"Fine." He takes his time thinking. Arrogance written on his face, he walks in a circle around me—assessing me. Trying to see what he can take from me. "Let's fight. One on one. You win, I let her go. You lose, I keep the girl and the knife."

"First of all, it's a dagger, not a knife." If he doesn't know that, he can't be a very good fighter. I've had years of training for this. "One on one. Fight until first blood. You've got yourself a deal."

I hold my hand out to shake his. He glances down at my hand, reaches out and tugs me forward so that I stumble to the ground. His grip is stronger than I had expected.

My nose is inches from the dirt and I find myself wondering why I am doing this. The faces of Saad, with his nose in an old children's book, and Aya, with her chubby cheeks that look like they're filled with marshmallows, come to mind. I'll keep getting up, for them.

He somehow has my dagger in his grip, coming at me. Rolling onto my back, I shove my foot against his shin and then again on the socket of his knee. There is a soft crack.

He grunts, shifting back so that my foot can't reach him. It gives me a chance to get back on my feet.

Everyone else watches, silent. The sound of my heavy breathing is all that can be heard. I grab the scimitar that is strapped across my back and hold it out. It has the advantage of reach, but it is less forceful.

It clashes against my dagger that he holds. I use the forward-back-forward-forward motion that we were trained to use. I should have never underestimated his strength, but his endurance is a different story.

He continues blocking my hits, but the strength it takes is wearing him down. His arms shake and sweat breaks on his forehead.

All I have to do is keep going, until he lets down his guard and I find a spot to get past his defences.

With each final hit, Rayan picks up on what I am planning and anger creases the lines between his brows. The harsh angles of his face are sharpened by the shadows that move when he moves. His nostrils flare, his eyes drifting behind me. "Kill her."

"No." I turn to look for the thief. As I do, Rayan swipes the dagger across my bicep—drawing blood. No.

In a way, fighting is a lot like love. In the beginning there is a lot of tension and emotions, and then after some time one side gets tired and gives up. Or someone cheats.

"Good fight." He wipes the blood on my dagger off using the hem of his shirt. "I will enjoy my gifts very much." When he looks at the thief, I get mad.

Angry enough to want to challenge him to the death. I was a fool to have fallen for his distraction trick.

His friends release Nawaz but not Alara. Nawaz comes up in front of Rayan, pulling the black bag off his head. "Let me fight you."

Rayan scoffs, taking his brothers good arm and tucking my dagger into his pocket to walk away. "Why would I choose to do that when I have already won? That's idiocy."

"I'll give you all the coins and gems that we carry with us." I thought my gamble was stupid, but Nawaz made it impossibly worse.

"Nawaz." My tone is a wary warning.

He glances over at me. "Look at her. I have to."

The thief. I asked her if she would cry, when I hurt her feelings earlier. She didn't. If there is any time for someone to cry, it would be now. Because I lost in the trade for her life.

She's not crying. It's worse than that. She has completely checked out. Her mind is miles away, to escape whatever she might have to endure with these men.

"Deal," Rayan says after consideration. "Beating the shit out of a spoilt prince will be fun."

His little brother tugs on Rayan's shirt. "What will you do with the girl? Let her go. No more fighting. I'm sorry for stealing." His voice is light and adorable, edged with the pain of his injury.

"Get back, kid. I win this, and you and mom never have to struggle or starve again." He steps forward, up to Nawaz, pulling my dagger out of his pocket. "Let's see if you bleed gold," he tells Nawaz, snarling. The hatred in his voice wounds oddly familiar to the way I would talk to Nawaz.

Already, in a swift movement, Nawaz disarms him. The dagger flies to the ground. "It's cute that you think you're going to find out."

Chapter 15

Alara: My body is pulled against something hard and warm. Large arms wrap around me, holding me close against their body.

For a moment, I let myself melt into the warmth and comfort of having someone hold me. It is a scary feeling, to enjoy something temporary.

But when every day has felt like walking through a barren desert, this feels like finding an oasis.

The smell of him is intoxicating and familiar. It makes my knees buckle, causing him to hold me closer. Disoriented, I place a hand against his hard chest and look up. Familiar eyes, now shades darker under the stars, stare back at me. "Zayen?"

He holds me closer, one hand gently sliding down my arm. "You're okay now." His voice is so kind, it is alarming. I don't trust it.

His touch causes a strange feeling in my chest that I obstinately ignore. I saw him lose the fight. Why am I in his arms? "What is going on?"

He looks away. "Nawaz won." He doesn't seem happy to admit it.

"He saved me? Is he okay?" I check around for Nawaz or Akilah, but there is nobody around. There is still a sharp pain on my neck, where blood was drawn.

His eyebrows lower. The shift is barely noticeable, but it darkens his expression. "He's fine." The word he is holding back is unfortunately.

This night has to be a fever dream. Maybe I passed out from exhaustion while walking down the mountain and in a little while I'm going to wake up with my face in the dirt.

That seems more realistic than this.

"Why am I . . . ?" In your arms? Alive? Alone with you?

My eyes unwillingly trail along his shoulder, down his biceps which are wrapped tightly around me. It makes my heart shiver. His shirt hugs against his body. My cheeks are a thousand times warmer than necessary.

Noticing the way I am looking at him, he loosens his grip on me and takes a small step back, to let me breath. The warmth of his body stays on my skin. It felt good to be hugged, even by him. "Akilah and Nawaz asked me to stay here with you while they went to get supplies."

He doesn't explain why he was holding me or why I do not remember anything happening after seeing blood being drawn from Zayen's arm. All I knew in that instant was that it was over for me, and that I hated feeling like an object to be traded.

"How dare you agree to that deal?" A searing anger seeps into my veins, like lava slipping through the cracks of a mountain, making my cheeks red for an entirely different reason. "You chose a knife over me?"

Although I wouldn't have expected less. I would have bet that he would trade my life for much less than that.

"A dagger," he corrects.

I turn on my heel, because if I keep looking at him I'll do something idiotic. There's a tightness in my chest, making it hard to breathe or think.

It's a feeling I haven't felt in a long time. Every day of my life has been the same. I've accepted the fate that my parents brought me—that I was destined to live every day by the skin of my teeth, fighting.

Having my life suddenly placed in someone else's hands, for them to gamble on it and lose, makes me hate him more with every breath.

"I'm not something to be sold or traded." I tangle my shaking fingers together, trying to remember what it feels like to feel anything but hate and anger. A few of my curls fall forward, brushing against my cheek.

"I never thought that you were." Zayen sighs behind me. His boots shuffle against the ground as he walks closer. With his hands on my arms, he turns me to face him. "You shouldn't have let those men capture you. You fight to the death, if you have to, before you ever let someone hold you captive. Because once they've got you, they can do anything to you."

I can't read his tense expression, but I want to know if there is a story behind his words. If there was a time where he made the mistake of being captured, and wished he has fought to the death.

I try to shrug out of his grip. "But it was five men against two of—"

He shakes his head, frustrated. "Even if it was you against a single man stronger than you, you would be at a technical disadvantage. But your mind is your strongest weapon. Use everything you've got and make sure that you either win, or die before you let that happen again. Do you understand?" When I don't respond, he raises an eyebrow.

I didn't think he would care. I shake my head, lowering my gaze to avoid the sandstorm in his eyes. "I'm not a warrior, like you. I'm only . . ." A thief. A daughter. A lonely girl from Wadi.

At that, he smiles. The soft curve of his lips have me staring. It softens the harshness of his features. "Of course you're a warrior. You fight every day to survive, don't you?"

His words are as unexpected as his smile. It makes me take a step back. His hands fall back to his sides. The warmth and kindness in his voice is like a hug. I want more of it—which makes it dangerous. "Why are you being nice to me? You hated me only an hour ago."

"I don't have to like you to be nice. I figured I should butter you up a little bit since I chose my dagger over you." I want to be angry at the reminder, but I no longer am. All I want is another one of his hugs. Clearly he is very good at 'buttering' me up.

"I appreciate your kindness."

"Yeah, well . . ." He shrugs, his head dipping to one side. It exposes the long, thick column of his neck. "It's a one time thing. Just don't get yourself in trouble again. Otherwise I'm going to have to put a leash on you." He smirks.

"Like a dog?" I exclaim.

He breathes in the night air and bites down on his lip to stop smiling wider. "The purpose of a leash is to indicate that you're mine, so that nobody else will try to take you." His lips have turned pink where his teeth had grazed.

I search for something hard to throw at him. On the floor, a silvery rock lies dormant. I lift it into my palm, throw it up into the air once and then launch it at him.

He ducks out of the way with a surprised laugh. It hits the mottled brown wall behind him. "You're stoning me, now?"

"You deserve to be punished." I glower at him.

At that he pauses, his gaze darkening. He is quick on his feet, mostly likely from his training, and unfortunately I find myself trapped in his grasp. "You want me to atone for my sins, Sariq?" I can't tell if it is anger lacing his tone, or something more dangerous than that. "I think you're the one that needs to be punished here."

Definitely more dangerous. "Is that why you look like you want to kill me all the time?" Or why he traded my life so easily.

This night could have ended very differently. I might have wished for death if I was with those men, wherever they would have taken me and whatever they would have done.

His lips part slowly as he considers his next words.

"We've got food!" a voice calls. "I think we need to find somewhere to sleep. Akilah disagrees, but we'll take a vote. I think she'll be outnumbered."

Nawaz carries a woven basket in his arms, filled to the brim with breads and fruits and some items that are wrapped tightly in soft papyrus.

Akilah carries a heavy, bulging satchel on her shoulder and a pouch of remaining coins in her hand. Her hair is now twisted into a bun at the nape of her neck.

I'm not sure if I am relieved to see them because I was afraid of what would happen next, or because of an entirely different reason.

"I can only agree to us taking a break for the night if we agree that there will be no more nightly stops until we reach Diyar," Akilah says, her voice smooth like honey. A complete contrast to her personality, it seems. "We do not have much time. The stone will not be easy to retrieve."

"Do you have to be so anal about everything?" Nawaz huffs, shifting the basket in his arms which makes his muscles flex. He has a tortured expression, as if he has just spent the last hundred years in a prison cell with Akilah.

Her eyes widen, her body rotating to face him. "Do not use that kind of language. Harsh speech is only acceptable for wrongful injustice, not for spoilt brats."

He glares. "You act as if you've known me for longer than, what, three days?"

"You can't even walk down a mountain without slipping on stray pebbles." She drops the heavy satchel at her feet when she reaches Zayen and I. It clatters loudly. "Clearly you have had no reason to worry about your survival, which is a privilege very few have." She eyes the basket full of food, as if that makes her point.

"So, where shall we stay for the night?" Nawaz asks, ignoring Akilah.

I would suggest my home, but it is not ideal sleeping conditions. I have a small couch and an old mat. It's an embarrassment—one that I am not ready to reveal to these people, who grew up in palaces and foreign lands.

It would be better if they could sleep somewhere else, then I can sneak out to find whatever it is my mom was talking about at home.

"Anyone in Wadi would offer their homes and their beds to the prince," I say. "People here are kinder than you'd expect." They always invite strangers to their homes, and prepare feasts as if they have endless amounts of money.

"If that is true, why didn't you offer us shelter in your home?" Zayen asks, folding his arms and watching me. That jolts my heart into a race.

I frown. How did you know?

I am not a fool. He raises an eyebrow.

I wish I could tie him up and continue stoning him. Or maybe I could buy some thread and sew his mouth shut permanently. It would make this journey much more tranquil.

I'd be mortified to see the pity on their faces when they see how I live.

"I thought you were from Diyar," Nawaz says, suspicion lacing his tone. His eyes roam my form with wariness, as if I am going to suddenly lash out and cut his throat.

Trust is such a strange thing. It can take lifetimes to gain and sentences to lose.

Zayen scoffs when I say nothing. "Don't believe everything you're told." His words sound like they hold more meaning than I know. "Her name isn't even Malaika."

I purse my lips to stop myself from swearing him. That was a truth that I was hoping I could conceal for a little while longer, at least until we reached Diyar.

Nobody makes me as unbelievably frustrated as this man beside me. The thoughts of what I wish to do to silence him are violent.

Zayen looks pleased with himself. He gestures forward with his hands. "Would you like to lead the way?"

I hate you.

CHAPTER 16

Z ayen: The thief bows her head in shame at my expression, and I quickly work to conceal my surprise.

The house is a rotting mess. Aside from the objects being carelessly thrown about—most likely when the guards came in to capture her mother—there are cracks in the walls and dirty dishes filling the sink. Every piece of furniture seems dusty and ancient.

I didn't know what to expect, but truly it wasn't this. Now it makes sense, the way she looked at the garden in the castle, and the bed she was given for the night, in amazement. Such simple things are actually the biggest privilege.

Nawaz, oblivious as always, asks, "Where's the bedroom?"

Alara seems to fold in on herself. Her arms cross over her stomach and her eyes shutter to the cracking tiled floor. She looks like she is ready to run to the bathroom to let out the contents of her stomach.

She doesn't have to be embarrassed about this, but I can see why she is. She had lead him to believe she was from a palace.

Now she has to admit that she does not own a bed. Her lies have come back to her, as they should.

"Sorry to break it to you." No, I'm not. "But you're sleeping on the floor, prince."

Nawaz seems to realise the stupidity of his question. He searches the thief's face for emotion, but she has concealed it well. "I'm sorry, I didn't mean to . . ." He searches for the words to console her, but there are none.

Her eyes shift to the ragged brown couch that is slightly torn at the arms. Her skin must feel like porcelain with the force she has to put into that tight-lipped smile now gracing her face. "You should take the couch. It's nothing near the comfort of your bed at home. I wish I could offer you more." At least there is truth in that.

He looks around the small house, at the mould in the corners of the roof and the tap-less sink, with a new perspective. I doubt he has ever been in a house like this. It's a good lesson. Maybe he will learn what reality is like for a lot of people. The world is a big place, with a lot of suffering. Not having a bed is the least of the problems in this land.

Because Saad and Aya don't have a proper bed. They don't have a home. They don't have parents. Some days, they don't have food. I hope they're okay.

There is a tightness in my chest as I imagine how they might feel—wondering why I left them with strangers and never even looked their way that day.

I wish I had gone to see them, because there is a chance that I may not make it back and they will never understand. There is also the chance that we might not get what the Hakeem wants.

I wonder how the Hakeem would do it. Would he force them to their knees and slice their throats? Would he leave them in a cage and 'forget' to feed them until they wasted away?

"I'll sleep on the floor," the thief offers. "I'm sorry. I—I'm sorry."

"Stop apologising." I hate that I want to hug her again. It felt surprisingly good to hold her in my arms. The way her body melted against mine. It made me feel protective of her. It was stupid. "It's not your fault. This is better than sleeping in a strangers house, or out in the dirt. We are grateful."

I look to the others for confirmation and they both nod. She really shouldn't be sorry. A starving man would not apologise for not having food to offer.

Her head is lowered but she looks up at me through her lashes, a few of her curls falling forward. The look in her eyes . . . Flip. I look away, worried about where my thoughts might lead me. "Let's just eat and get to bed."

~~*~~

When I wake up, the sun hasn't risen yet. The air is still cool and damp, making me shift in the blanket I am wrapped in. I use the satchel that Akilah bought as a pillow.

I read somewhere that way back in the past, before plush pillows existed, the wealthier families would sleep on stone head rests and it was solely to keep bugs from crawling into their ears. I will be grateful that I do not have to sleep with my head on stone.

Soft whispers alert my brain, making me sit up. There is no lock on the door. Anyone can come in, including that kid's brother.

Rising to my feet silently, I follow the hushed sounds until I find the only room in the house. It's small, filled with stacked books and old boxes. My footsteps are silent—I'd like to say I am like a stealthy ninja, of course—and neither of them detect my presence.

The thief sits on one of the boxes. Nawaz stands in front of her. From certain angles, what they are doing could look like something unspeakable. Something that only Nawaz, the unfeeling sinner, would do.

But from the door I can see that he is only tilting her chin up, gently tucking her hair behind her ear. He couldn't possibly care about her.

Most likely, he wants to redeem his reward for winning the fight for her.

"So what did you tell me that wasn't a lie?" he asks, his voice dancing with the dark.

This I'd like to hear.

"Well . . ." She tries to lower her gaze.

He kneels down in front of her. Something a prince should never do for anyone. The Hakeem would chastise him for it—and would go ballistic if he knew his son slept on the floor like a commoner. "The truth, please."

"I'm not royalty, my name isn't Malaika and I'm not interested in winning your affection. I believe everything I told you was un-true. Your father offered me money and hopefully now that you see where I live, you understand why I accepted it. I shouldn't have lied." Her words come tumbling out of her mouth faster than normal.

He nods slowly. "And . . . Why does Zayen call you a sariq?" A thief. Because she is one.

"Because that is what I am." Now her voice is so filled with shame that she has lowered her pitch, making it hard to hear her. "I go to the souk and steal. That's how I have survived up until now." She's really laying everything out in the open now. Maybe she has learnt her lesson.

Here is another reality check for the prince, that the world is not a fairytale. That many people suffer; many people do bad things to survive.

"What you did is wrong," he says. His point is true, yet it is ironic coming from him. He needs to hear his own words. He used to send guards down to beat me, and yet he has the audacity—

There is a swarming feeling in my head that clouds my thoughts and makes me what to blindly punch everything that gets in my way. Frustration.

My fists tighten at my sides. Now is not the time to get into another fight. If I did, though, he would have no guards to hide behind this time. I'll wait until a moment where it'll hurt him the most, then I will strike.

He wasn't always like this. There were days that I remember vaguely, where he would let me lead him everywhere, waddling after me and repeating everything that I did. There were days were we would laugh and play, until he realised who he was and the power went to his head. Just like his father. Our father.

"And you don't have feelings for Zayen?" he asks.

She shakes her head. Now any interest that Nawaz may have shown will vanish. The only toys he likes playing with are ones that other people want.

He is silent for a long time. There is a heavy silence in the air. He carries every bit of power that has been placed on his shoulders. No matter where he goes, he stands tall. If nothing else, he plays the part of a prince well.

"It is in our past now," Nawaz says. "We are on an unknown journey. When things are out of our control, the one thing we can choose is who we are. That's the fun of life, laa? We can recreate ourselves as many times as we wish."

He is trying to use words to seem deep and meaningful, but he is as deep as an evaporating puddle under the desert sun.

She nods, shifting to the edge of the box as if she wants him to continue talking the way he is. Like that is her dirty talk. "Who do you want to be?" Her voice is gentler than normal.

I'm sick of this. Clearly he is telling her what she wants to hear. That's one thing he is good at: sweet talking. It is why I will never trust him.

Heading back into the main area the of the thief's home, I grab some coins from the pouch resting on the tattered arm of the couch. It is right above Akilah's head.

When she doesn't wake up at the sound of shifting coins, I gently place the pouch back down and step out into the night. The darkness is consuming. All of the torches have been extinguished to avoid setting the homes on fire. My only guide is the stars and the moon, that create the softest glow on the compact sand below my feet.

Each breath I take and movement I make is echoed in the heavy silence. There was life flowing through these streets only hours ago, and now it is deserted.

I lean back against the clay wall of one of the houses and stare up at the sky. The stars in the shape of a triangle point towards Qadura. It is how they decided that it would be the the capital city—chosen by the stars.

Sometimes when I'm looking at the stars, or feeling raindrops kissing my cheeks, or reading a good novel, I find myself wondering who else is experiencing the same thing. Because even when we are completely alone, each moment is still shared.

I have slept longer than three hours. It's longer than I have slept in years. Most nights, I'd be with Saad and Aya by now, and then would be abruptly woken from a fake slumber to face Nawaz's guards wrath.

I'm not used to being idle, and I don't want to be. Purpose is the only reason we watch the sun rise and fall; the only reason we put one foot in front of the other.

And now, I don't know what lies ahead. Everything feels uncertain and foreign, but I can't turn away from it.

After what must be an hour of walking, and searching, I find a stable. It is connected to a house, and there is a small space behind it where crops are growing.

The horses nicker and stomp when the wooden doors squeak open. Sitting inside, along with his friends, is Rayan.

They're all playing a game of Khara Cards. I hold my breath, not knowing what move to make next. This is not a good situation to be in, but I stand my ground as they all rise to stand with their eyes set on me.

I need to make it look like I walked in here to find him on purpose. "I have come to buy your horses."

"You come to my home and make requests?" He cracks his neck. The sound seems to echo. "You're not leaving this place with anything other than a broken body." His tone is venomous.

CHAPTER 17

Alara: Zayen is gone, along with some of the money that we had remaining.

"We have to carry on without him," Akilah says, packing everything back into an overfilled satchel. "We don't have time to search for him."

Nawaz shrugs and pushes open the front door of my home. The door nearly comes off it's hinges as it opens.

It doesn't make sense that Zayen would run off without a reason. He cares about those kids, which means it's unlikely he would walk away like this.

Something has to be wrong. "We should look for him," I say.

Akilah shakes her head, following Nawaz out the door. "We have no clues to where he went. It would be foolish to waste time like that."

I glance back over the inside of my house, searching for any sign of him. It all looks exactly the same, untouched. She's right—he left no note, no signs, nothing for us to follow. He either ditched us, or made an unbelievably stupid move.

"We should leave a note for him. In case he comes back."

"Do as you wish," Akilah says, not stopping. I don't understand why she is in such a rush. It's not like any of her loved ones are trapped in a castle with guards ready to let them drop dead at a words notice.

With a deep sigh, I lift my own small bag of items to carry with me and step out into the heat of the sun.

Maybe if I knew more about Akilah, I'd feel relaxed around her. I don't know where she is taking us, I don't know what her values are and I don't know who she works for. There is nothing that I know about her, besides her name. She could be lying about that, too.

Freeing me from prison was a kind gesture that could have been done purposefully, for her own benefit—because she is now armed with a prince. He is worth a lot. Nothing is stopping her from betraying us. She has no reason to give the stone over, except that she gave her word.

I pause in my tracks. She seems more in a rush now that the one guard, who was sent to protect Nawaz, is gone. This is suspicious.

But I am not on good enough terms with the prince to tell him not to trust her, or not to follow her. The Hakeem seemed to believe she would return.

I guess I will have to be the one to make sure nothing happens to him now.

"Think I'd give up that easily?" A voice calls out, his tone so rough that I almost don't recognise it.

He—My heart stretches when my eyes find him. There are cuts and bruises on his bare arms. His hair is damp and there is another cut on his temple that he doesn't seem bothered by, even though it is still damp with blood.

"What did you do?" Nawaz asks. His tone is more curious than concerned. It's a bit sad that the future leader of our land has so little empathy. But when have our leaders ever been good?

Zayen now wears a checkered black and white keffiyeh on his head, folded and tied at the back like a bandana. It seems to have slowed some of the bleeding.

"I brought transport." He tilts his head back, nodding towards the three horses that are following behind him. Their hooves step in sync, creating a calming rhythm as they walk.

He is grinning, proud of himself, even though he can barely walk straight and is losing a lot of blood.

"I think we should play a game called 'how many fights can Zayen lose on this journey'," Nawaz says.

"A thank you would be nice." He wipes some of the blood off his face with the back of his hand. "And I won. I will train, to make sure I keep winning."

"Shukran." Nawaz nods.

Zayen stares. "Did you just—? Wait, I think my ears were blocked. Can you repeat—?"

Nawaz grins, which is rather unlike him. It suits him. That smile that could dazzle the stars.

My fingers wrap around Zayen's wrist and I lead him towards our neighbours house. He follows me without any resistance, which is unusual because he always seems on edge.

That makes me trust him less. Not that I trusted him much in the first place. And with Akilah's position, and the fact that

Nawaz is the prince, means that there is nobody here that seems trustworthy.

This seems like the perfect recipe for great teamwork and success.

When we reach my neighbours front door, curiosity gets the best of me. I release his wrist and shake my head. "I don't get it. Why haven't you asked where I am taking you?"

He blows air out of his nose in what must be a laugh, then looks me over. His eyes trail over me slowly. "You're too small to cause much damage."

Does he not remember me throwing stones at him last night? It's fair that I am not much of a combat fighter, but I could do damage.

To prove it, I use my talents as a thief and snatch his precious blade from his pocket with ease. I am ready to taunt him with it. Except that it is slick with a sticky red liquid.

"Whose..." Maybe I don't want to know. Did he hurt someone innocent? Is that how he got the horses, by killing the owner?

He lifts his hand to run it through his hair, then remembers it's coated in blood and stops himself. "Don't look at me like that." His hand falls to his side and he huffs, walking past me to enter our neighbours home.

His house is in similar condition to ours, except there is some new furniture and the inside seems to have a fresh coat of paint. He must have used the coins I gave him for taking care of my mama to do it—not that he took care of my mama when it mattered.

The old man, Abbas, stands, his knees shaking as he does. His hands wave out in front of him, shooing us away. "No, girl. No more. The-The guards coming to your home. That wasn't the deal. No more." He looks over at Zayen—tall, broad-shouldered and definitely a guard as well. "Leave."

"Please, we only need your aid." I gesture to Zayen's head. "We have given you water from our taps for years. Please don't let my friend suffer. He has been hurt."

He swallows, causing his hollow, sagging cheeks to concave. "I have a kit." He points a shaky kit towards the bathroom. "Take it and leave."

The bathroom doesn't have a door. The walls have begun to turn brown and mouldy. It makes me feel deeply sad, because I wish to help him more.

When I turn to Zayen, I am surprised to read the same expression on his face. He wants to help this man that he hasn't known for more than two minutes.

I push the kit into his bleeding hands. Maybe it is just me reading into things wrong again. After everything he has done, I am not going to allow myself to believe he is good based on a fleeting expression.

He follows me out Abbas' house, thanking him profusely. Nawaz and Akilah have made use of their time by setting up the horses for travel.

I take a bucket of water and cloth into my home. The door groans, and Zayen mutters 'same' under his breath.

He sits on the arm of the couch as I collect what I need to clean him up.

In this moment, it feels good to be useful. It's a feeling I haven't felt in a long time, because all I have been able to do is not die in a world designed to kill me.

It fills a small part of the hollowness inside me, that wonders what I try to survive for.

"Take off your shirt." It also feels good to be able to tell someone what to do, especially someone who grew up in a palace and has muscles that could crush me.

He shakes his head, sensing that I am enjoying it, but complies none the less. His hand goes up to the hem of his rough white shirt and he pulls it over his head in a swift movement, tossing it to the side.

Oh. My gaze goes up to the cracking ceiling, then down to the dusty floors. There's a wild racing in my chest. I'm going to have to look at him at some point. I've seen a bare chest before, but not his. It slipped my mind that as a trained royal guard he would be like. . . this. Impressive.

His chest, his shoulders. Every part of him chiselled from years of training to protect royalty.

"Why is your hair damp?" I try to fill the silence and my curiosity. In the dim light, his hair seems darker. What I really want to ask is where he went, and what he did, and whose blood is coating his weapons.

"Because I'm an idiot who thought I'd try to be useful." There's a red flush to his cheeks, but it could be smeared blood.

I take the cloth and begin wiping the edges of the wounds on his temple and his arms. The muscles in his arms tense, emphasising the veins running down to his wrists. Blood soaks into the cloth quickly and I have to wring it out a few times.

There is a paste in the kit made of a green herb substance. I remember mama using it on me as a child, whenever I fell.

The time I remember the clearest was when I was running on the beach one afternoon, against my fathers wishes. The sand was sparkling gold beneath my feet. Salty air had whipped my curls away from my face. It had felt so freeing, that for a moment, I closed my eyes.

And tripped over a rock. Lucky girl that I am, I hit my head and the blood had gushed out so profusely that I could barely see.

Mama had pressed this paste into my wounds, and while my vision was still dotted with black, I knew from her gentle touch that I would be okay.

It ended up being a great day, because I got frozen strawberry-flavoured cream afterwards. Probably because I needed sugar or I'd pass out

As I apply the paste to Zayen's wounds, he flinches. Small lines form between his thick eyebrows. His jaw tenses, his fingers digging into the side of my couch, turning them white at the tips.

He holds onto my wrists when I accidentally press too hard on his temple. "Stop enjoying this, you sadist." His voice is ragged.

"I'm not." I smile, looking up at him through my lashes.

"Could I ask you something?" His eyes darken. He leans in dangerously close to me, and suddenly it feels like I can see the pain of what he went through swimming in his eyes. Not only from today, but from years and years of being hurt.

"You can ask. I might not answer." That's a fair deal, since he has satisfied none of my curiosity.

Still holding me, he asks, "Do you consider me weak for what happened last night? For . . . losing the fight." His chest seems to stop moving, as if he is holding his breath.

His question, the vulnerability in it, makes me move in closer; makes me want to hug him. His grip on me loosens and his expressions changes, probably realising he showed me more than he might have wanted to.

I remember how staggering his grip was, from the multiple times he got tired of me and roughly grabbed me. The force of his strength could easily break me.

"Weak is the last thing I would describe you as. Everyone loses battles sometimes. I've never fought in my life but last night, you said I was a fighter. It's all about context. I think you're . . ." Realising I am only inflating his ego unnecessarily, I change my wording. "You're not bad."

"Not bad." He smiles, knowing that wasn't what I was going to say. "Have you ever kissed anyone?" That sends a jolt to my chest. I wasn't expecting—Why does he care?

"This isn't the playground. Why are you asking such insignificant questions?"

"I don't know . . ." He lifts his broad, very bare, shoulders, shrugging. He must have searched for a quick change to the topic, and this definitely changed it. "I guess it would just be a shame if you haven't, because it's enjoyable."

"Enjoyable." The sound that that comes out of my nose is definitely not attractive. "I doubt that."

I unwrap the kiffyeh from his head and re-tie it properly for him. I've seen boys do it here in Wadi and I've always wanted to do it for someone. Although when I'd imagined it, I imagined doing it for the man I'd spend my life with.

His eyes follow my every move. He glances at my lips, which makes me wrap the piece of cloth around his head a little tighter then necessary.

This behaviour may be part of a game plan. I still haven't forgotten the words he spoke to me the day before we left. I'm going to make sure you wish you had never stepped foot inside the palace.

I'd be a fool to forget that warning. Every move he makes could be with that intention. He was trained to be a man of strategy, and so I may be walking through a minefield without knowing it.

But with the way he is looking in my direction, it makes me want to be reckless for only a moment. To see if anything besides food could be considered 'enjoyable'.

"Time to go!" Akilah calls, pushing open the door. It bangs against the wall. She has lost her patience—what little of it there was.

I nod, dusting my hands and repacking everything into the kit. Glancing back at Zayen, he is still leaning against the arm of the couch with his eyes on me. There's a sly smile on his face.

"What is going on with you? We're you drugged or something?" He seems too calm. It's unnerving.

That seems to amuse him even more. He holds his arms out. "Everything happens so fast, doesn't it? I've never lived my life like this, with no idea what tomorrow will be like. I figured it would be better to embrace it than fight it."

That's the complete opposite of how my life has been. I've always stepped out of my front door, wondering if I'd step back in.

Sensing that he would dodge any further questions I have lingering on my tongue, I decide not to prod. "I don't believe that you could come back a different person. I think you're faking this whole . . . act." I gesture to him, to how relaxed he looks.

"Well, I guess you'll have to wait and see." His fingers slip into my hair, roughly shaking up my curls, and he walks out without a glance back.

My face scrunches and I try to reorganise myself before stepping out into the bright, scorching sun.

All three of them have already mounted their horses, leaving me to decide which one of them I would want to share a horse with.

I haven't ridden a horse in many, many years but I can predict that riding with Akilah will not be fun. She is going to go fast, which will make this an unbelievably uncomfortable journey.

Then there is Zayen, who is behaving very strangely. He had murder in his gaze only a day ago, and I don't doubt that he may try to push me off the horse if I let my guard down.

So I step up to Nawaz's horse and hold my hand out for him to help me up. He does, with a pleased smile. His bronze skin seems to glow in the sunlight.

I glance back at Zayen who doesn't seem so happy about my choice. He must be sad that it'll be harder to hurt me at such a distance.

"Yalla," Akilah calls, already a good distance ahead.

The calm before the storm.

Chapter 18

Zayen: The area we are about to pass through is dangerous. We are going to have to keep our guard up.

Many people spread rumours about what happens to those who go through Ardifa. It's an abandoned land that not many people come back from, between Wadi and Diyar.

The rumours are as bad, if not worse, than the rumours about the prison in the palace. All taped about people getting captured, tortured—their fingernails being removed from their hands and shoved into their eyeballs.

Told in jest, but certainly not a joke.

The woods here are thick with trees, so closely huddled together that it is hard to see a clear path. Their leaves create canopies above my head that dance in the breeze.

The lack of birdsong rings alarm bells in my head. There should be signs of life, but there isn't.

My legs have begun to feel numb. We have been riding non-stop, because Akilah is relentless. It's been hours, but it feels like weeks. My back needs to be twisted and massaged by one of the royal servants. The cuts and bruises lining my body don't help.

But I won. They had tried to drown me but, this time, I won. My jaw clenches at the reminder of what it felt like to lose. I just want to go to war—I want to fight over and over in order to prove myself again.

My grip tightens on the reigns and my horse, irritated, nods it's head to try and get me to loosen up. She's a beautiful horse—her brown and white coat shines, reflecting the love and care given to her.

I wonder if this horse belongs to that little boy. If he is the one who took care of her. He must have walked into the stables, searching for his brother and found—

How would their mother feel, knowing she couldn't protect her children? Knowing that it could have ended much worse if I had twisted my dagger a little deeper—

I left coins behind in exchange for their horses, more than enough, but damage has been done in ways that can never be reversed. All because I thought, stupidly, that I'd try and be a hero.

A deep, throaty groan leaves my lips. I hate the feeling of frustration and anger building in my chest.

The thief doesn't even know me and yet she is right, my calmness is an act. Beneath the surface I am bubbling with a rage that unlocked the moment I lost that fight. It has never happened before.

I thought that maybe flirting with her, getting some sort of reaction, would take my mind off things. But it didn't.

"Are your wounds still bleeding or causing pain?" the thief asks, her head turned back to look at me.

She shows genuine concern for me, and I am not sure why. She even cleaned up, albeit roughly, my wounds for me. Nobody has done that before. I've done nothing but gamble on her life and degrade her.

"I'm fine." At least I am good at pretending to be. As long as I can keep going without blacking out, I will be fine.

A growl pierces the air.

Not now.

All three horses come to a halt, their hooves knocking against the ground in anxious anticipation. Air blows out of their nostrils, filling the eerie quiet. They're not sure what to do or what direction to run in.

"Akilah, what do we do?" Nawaz asks. His green jewelled eyes are assessing, like a leopard's, for further signs of movement.

"There's only one thing to do." She knocks the stirrup against her horse's side and holds onto her reigns. "Run."

Her horse is gone in an instant, rustling bushes are the only remnant of her. Nawaz and I take a second before we are close on her tail.

But there is a heavy thumping behind us. Something that I hope we never see, because if we do we would have to fight it off. Fighting wild animals has been a part of my training as a royal guard, we had to practice on wild cats. It was the hardest training of my life.

I might have given up, if my father wasn't watching me and waiting for me to prove myself as a disappointment.

Fighting an unknown wild animal while injured and barely armed would be a disaster.

I dip my body forward, avoiding low-hanging branches that threaten to hit me in the face. A couple of them catch my bare arms, causing my previous wounds to burn.

It's hard to gallop when feeling so tense. The art of riding a horse at full speed is to let go of control completely, to let the animal do what it does best, but it's much harder when there is the high chance something will go wrong.

I glance back over my shoulder to see if any hint of what is chasing us could be seen. The bushes and trees are still, only gently swaying.

It only heightens my unease, not knowing where it might have gone.

My horse snorts when I knock stirrup against it's side. Reluctantly, it speeds up and soon I find myself riding beside Akilah.

She glances over at me. Her straight, dark hair creates a shadow behind her as it dances with the wind. Sweat beads her forehead. Her eyes remain fierce and unreadable.

I find my gaze wondering down to her chest which rises and falls with the movement of her horse. Tearing my eyes away, I ask, "What now?"

"There's a house," she explains, not looking at me. Her guard is up as she searches for the creature.

That doesn't sound like a good idea in a place like this. Not with all the rumours here. "How do you know that?" I don't trust her for a second.

Especially because she doesn't sound breathless either, which indicates she is fit and trained. It only further proves how little I know about her.

She shakes her head, speeding up to stay ahead of me. "Follow me or keep running until you find somewhere better to stop. Your choice."

This could be a set up.

If I had to choose between death and being captured, I will always choose death. Just like I told the thief, there are things much worse than death.

But Akilah is right. What other option is there?

My eyes meet Nawaz's over my right shoulder. The thief is holding onto him, so tight that it seems intimate. But it's more likely fear. She's the only one that seems out of breath.

The image of her holding onto him brings back memories of Nawaz earlier in the year. He had figured out who it was that I found attractive, and made it his mission to win her over. Arayana. She was more kind than she was beautiful, and she was strikingly beautiful. He was successful, and made sure to time it so that I would walk in at the moment she was unraveling.

That anger only spurs me to go faster, until I can't think about anything except the sting of the wind in my eyes.

We come to the end of the tree line, with Akilah in the lead, where green hills roll out and nothing but a sprinkling of trees and tiny yellow flowers can be seen.

We make it only ten or so meters out when that same animalistic roar follows us and the bushes part. My horse is going so fast that it is impossible to turn around and see the creature, not without throwing off my balance.

Akilah begins to swerve her horse to the side, going at an angle towards a large hill. Nearing it, a cave-like hole becomes visible. It's not very tall, and I'd likely have to duck against my horse to fit in, but it seems like our only shot.

Akilah ducks, holding tightly against her horse as she disappears into the darkness of the cave.

As soon as all three horses are in, Akilah throws a leg back and slips off her horse, her entire body slamming against the dirt wall and she pushes a button and a large cage-like gate slams down.

A loud scream follows a thump. Through the gates, two shadows struggle. One is much larger than the other.

"Who—?" I slip off my horse and search for Nawaz, but his eyes are wide in fear and directed towards the two figures outside the gate.

"Alara. She . . . She fell." He doesn't blink. His body is still. "I . . . It was too late. The horse wouldn't—"

Alara's screams fill the air, drowning out any excuse Nawaz was about to make.

One thing I know is that he didn't push her. He wouldn't purposely kill anyone he has a chance of sleeping with.

I can't let her die. "Open the gate." The creature seems to be dragging her limp body. But the lighting inside the cave makes it too dark to confirm.

"No," Akilah says, moving her body to block the button. "There could be more of them."

"It's my duty." I have to protect her. It's what I was raised and trained to do.

I walk up to Akilah. My body towers over her. I have the advantage of height and strength. Nothing is going to stop me.

She stares up at me, her body automatically preparing to fight. She positions one foot in front of the other, her stance seeming to have admittedly good form. "I'm not going to let you be an idiot."

"Don't act like you care about me." I pull out my dagger. The promise I made to myself is that I would not lose another fight.

I won't.

CHAPTER 19

Alara: Die before you get captured.

The thick, heavy smell of smoke and roasting meat fills my nose. My body feels as if it has been stomped on by a dozen horses.

Zayen's words—once they've got you, they can do anything to you—repeats itself over and over in my head. But louder than his word, is my own, chastising me for my stupidity.

My body can not move, not only because of its numbness but because I have been chained with a cold material.

Stupid, stupid, stupid. Tears threaten to break out of my closed eyes. Curiosity had gotten the best of me, and I had turned in the direction of whatever was chasing us.

As soon as I had, my balance was lost and I fell. We were so close to being safe.

But I had seen what was chasing us. I saw it as I laid on the grass near the hill, my body feeling like it was broken. I saw it as it lifted me and slammed me back against the dirt.

It wasn't a creature. It wasn't an animal. Or a monster.

It was a man.

A man who tied a cloth around my eyes and dragged me, with a painfully strong grip, across the grass until my body and brain went numb.

My limbs shift and pull against my shackles. They're tight, feeling like they're biting against my wrists and ankles. I can't move an inch. I am stuck against the wall, arms hanging up vertically to my shoulders. The position makes me feel unbelievably vulnerable.

The cloth over my eyes makes it impossible to figure out where I am. There is no chance I have of getting out of here—wherever here is. I am not a princess. I'm nothing. A nobody. There is nothing worth saving.

But my mother is worth saving. So I will try to stay alive, for her.

The cloth is pulled from my eyes. I barely have time to adjust to the light as I come face-to-face with the same man who chased and dragged me away. His body is more bear-like than human. There are dark markings, similar to henna but much darker, where his hair should be.

He could easily be mistaken for an animal, with his size and the terrifying expression on his face—and his green tinted skin.

If I could move back, if I could move at all, I would. My heart beats in my throat. My entire body is heavy, like it has been filled with stones.

It is a cavernous room. The walls are all jagged rock. There's barely any light, aside from a hole high up in the ceiling.

"Wha—" I have to stifle a sob. There is a question on my lips that I don't want to ask; that I don't want the answer to. "What do you want?" My lips shake as though I have been sitting in an ice bath for hours.

His eyes roam my face. Large hands, big enough to cover my entire face, reach out and brush dirt off my face. I flinch, my head twisting to the side. A shiver dances down my spine.

"Afraid." His voice sounds like how I'd imagine someone who hasn't spoken in years would sound. It is savage. His hand goes down to my throat and squeezes. It makes it impossible to breathe. I squirm. "Weak."

"Don't." My voice is strained. I'm not going to beg a man that seems to barely be able to speak.

He shoves my head back, knocking it against a ragged stone wall. "Don't tell me what to do!" My eyes squeeze shut as a sudden ringing fills my ears.

"What do you want?" I scream back, but it only makes my head hurt more. Please don't kill me.

Although I'm sure the rest of the group have left me behind anyways. They're probably closer to Diyar now, knowing that I won't last long here.

"Nothing." And that may be the most dangerous answer.

But everyone always has something that they desire. Not that I have anything to offer.

His face moves in close. He seems curious, like he has never seen anything like me. When his face dips closer to my neck, he breathes me in like I am a candle filled with scented oil.

He pulls something out of his pocket. A piece of wood, carved into a sharp edge. "You break easy?" The question makes me suck in a deep breath, but my lungs still feel empty of air.

This is what Zayen was talking about. That it's better to die than be captured. Now, this man, if I can even call him that, can do whatever. I have no power, nothing to bargain with, and no weapons.

I still have the cut on my neck from when I allowed myself to be captured before. There's a saying that life will keep sending lessons until you learn. This feels like a lesson, I just didn't know I would face it again so soon.

There is a response on my tongue again. No. But if I say that, he would want to test me. If I said yes . . . I believe he would try, anyways.

He grunts, waiting for a response. I simply tilt my chin up, not willing to back down.

He grabs the back of my hair with one hand, his fist pulling my head. The place where he had previously knocked my head sears with a blinding pain.

His other hand lifts his make-shift knife to my cheek. "Answer me."

Shedding tears is as pointless as screaming. "Unchain me and find out." I've managed to survive so far, under unlikely circumstances.

"That would be stupid."

That is true. I tilt my head to the side, and a few of my curls brush against my face. "Come on, at least one hand? You really think this tiny girl has a chance against you? Do you not think yourself good enough to win?" Hitting his ego could work.

"No." He grunts.

Or not.

I assess his stance. He is kneeling close to me, his hand still holding my hair back. But he hasn't noticed that the wooden blade he holds is pointed upwards.

It could be a risk. No, it is definitely a risk. But it may be the only chance I get.

I clench my core upwards, using the chains on my wrists as leverage, and knock the front of my hip up against the weapon in his hands.

It lacerates his skin and he gasps, immediately pulling it out. Seeing the gash nearly makes me puke as blood immediately replaces the space where the knife was.

He growls, his fist coming up fast and slamming into my stomach. It knocks every bit of air out of my body, leaving me wheezing. It rises again and I don't bother to ask him to stop. I bite down on my lip to stop making a sound from the blinding pain that it causes when he hits the same spot twice.

The force of it causes the chains on my wrists to tug upwards, nearly dislocating my wrists. Shuddering breaths leave my lips.

Physical pain is thankfully something I have not had a lot of experience with. Being someone from a small, poor village, I have had no reason to be in a fight. Most people attack when they want something. Which is why I don't understand why this beast of a man is doing this.

"Stupid!" He roars. His fist comes up again, and I brace myself. I knew injuring him was a risk. I'd do it again.

Closing my eyes and blocking out small stream of light, a soft gasp leaves my lips as his fist comes down, this time on my thigh. The pain makes me want to cry, even while knowing it won't do anything. I still wish to have something as an outlet or distraction.

My body remains still, eyes falling closed. Enough. I've had enough. I rest my head back, causing the place where it slammed against the wall to throb.

And it makes me incredibly frustrated to know that it's not in my hands to stop it from happening. I lost control the moment my balance had thrown me from the horse and I was captured.

A swift swooshing sound is followed by a disgusting squelch. It makes my eyes fly open, my heart jumping for a moment in fear of the unknown.

The man drops down to the side. As his head slides cleanly off his neck all I can feel is grateful that he didn't fall on top of me. Blood begins to pool into a puddle, and I can't shift away from it.

It is hard for my eyes to stray from the deep red that seeps out of the giant man's severed head, even as footsteps draw closer.

When I look up, I am regrettably relieved to see Zayen staring back at me. I can't believe the look in his eyes.

"Are you serious?" I say through gritted teeth. All I can feel is pain coursing through my body.

He states at me. The look—he seems attracted to seeing me in chains. I want to slap him, even though he saved me from further pain.

There is a puddle of blood nearly touching my leg and he has the audacity—"Get me out!" In the cave, my words seem to echo up to the small stream of light.

He walks to me, all muscles and height. His dagger lays at his waist, as usual, with his longer scimitar laying on the floor, coated in blood.

A part of me wants to reach out for him, to drag my hands across his broad chest and make sure he is real.

When he kneels, I meet his gaze. My lungs feel like they are finally able to function. My heart, however, seems out of control.

I can't believe he cared.

"Say please." His gaze trails to my bound wrists, then down my arms to my neck and collarbone.

I tug at the chains, causing them to ache deeply. My hands have begun to tingle with the lack of blood flow. "This is not funny! Get me out." Anger flares through me. He is taking this too lightly. "What, is this some kind of fantasy of yours?"

He doesn't respond. His gaze doesn't go lower than my upper chest, thankfully.

"My saviour, everyone," I say, even though we are alone. The thought crosses my mind again, that we are alone. He could do anything. He wouldn't, would he?

For some reason, he is able to read that. "You think I would harm you?" His gaze flashes with unsaid words, before he lowers his gaze.

I try to conceal my expression, my gaze lowering again to the pool of blood. It has stopped growing in size. I glance at the head that lies on its side. Dark, haunted eyes still open and staring at me.

A deep sigh is followed by Zayen trekking through the blood puddle and to the decapitated body. He feels up the body, checking pockets and crevices. "I told you—"

"Not to get captured. I know."

He looks up at me as he pulls out a thin silver chain with a set of keys. "Do you understand now?"

He then wipes his sword against the man's clothing, removing the blood, before sheathing it on his back.

"I fought," I tell him. Would he be proud of me for that?

"You need to fight better." I guess not. It's not like I needed approval from him.

"Did you not see how huge he was?"

"Size doesn't matter." It definitely matters. "The best way to win a fight is to not let your opponent know it's a fight."

I tug at my bindings, hoping that will indicate that I want to be let out. If that was not obvious enough already.

"Come on, please let me out. I'm tired and my body hurts." Like I have been dragged through the mud, which is quite literal.

I think he must hear from the tone of my voice how drained I feel. He shifts closer to me and begins unlocking the chains on my ankle. His eyes keep lifting to mine, gaging my reaction. "What did he want?"

The release of pressure on my ankles makes a small whimper leave my lips. I can't imagine how good it'll feel for my hands to not be hanging up on the wall.

"Why did you come?" I don't understand.

He shifts over to my side, getting so close that I can smell his oud. It's spicy and warm, the comfort of it makes me imagine what it would be like to lay at his side with his big arms around me. The warmth of his skin against mine would make me forget about the world.

I flinch back, shocked by my own thoughts.

One of my hands drops back to my side, numb. But I watch the shift in his face when his eyes meet mine, those warm brown eyes trying to read me. "Do you truly believe I would hurt you, Alara?"

Why is he not calling me Sariq, like he usually does? Is it a tactic to make me believe that I can trust him? Well, I don't.

That is not why I was flinching, but it doesn't matter. "You said it yourself, 'the best way to win a fight is to not let your opponent know it's a fight'. I will not let my guard down around you."

"If I wanted to hurt you, I would have just left you to die here. Use your—" He turns his face, trying to control his frustration. His jaw hardens.

It's hard to dismiss how striking he is. With his thick eyebrows framing those unfairly long lashes. His nose is masculine and structured, but then his lips are—no.

In silence, he returns to his task and unchains my other wrist. It flops back to my side like a dead fish. There is no feeling in my arms, which I hadn't realised until now.

"Come," he says, rising back to his feet.

No.

CHAPTER 20

Z ayen: "Why not?"

She glares at me, as if I didn't help her by stopping her from being hurt further by whoever that man—if I can call him a man—was. "Because you didn't say please."

"Oh, looks like getting the shit beaten out of you has taught you sarcasm."

She looks me over. "You would know."

"Ouch." That's kind of funny.

Maybe I should just leave her here. I don't know what I was thinking, trying to be a hero.

I sigh and the sound seems to rumble off the walls. "Fine, be a brat." I'll leave her. She can find her own way. Maybe Akilah was right. I wasted my time.

"Wait." Her voice comes out softer, more vulnerable. I stop, already half way out the carved entrance, but don't turn to face her. "I can't. . ." Her words come out shaky. "I can't move. Everything feels numb. I can't."

I'm an idiot for feeling sympathy towards her. But she just sounds so sweet and—I turn to her, keeping my expression hard.

"Give me one good reason why I shouldn't leave you here for the wolves," I demand.

Her eyes widen and she tries to push herself up to her feet, only for her arms to give out. "Wolves?" Her throat seems to be closing up.

I don't know if there are wolves. None of the stories about Ardifa have actually been confirmed. But if there are giant men with eyes as black as the depths of the ocean, then wolves sure are a possibility.

"Give me a reason."

"I . . ." She seems to struggle to come up with one. "I can't let her die because of me." Her big brown eyes seem to shine, the light from above falling on her like it is drawn towards her.

Her mother. She's playing the sympathy card. It's the only reason she is here, doing this. That is the one, probably the only, thing we have in common.

"One condition."

She manages to lift her arm to the back of her head and lightly presses it, wincing as she does. "What?"

"If I don't make it back for any reason, promise me you'll take care of Saad and Aya." I step back into the dim cave. My eyes trail away to the man whose skin has begun to go a greyish colour. Do that, and I'll protect you with my life for as long as I can."

"Saad and Aya. Those kids?" she asks, her gaze following mine to the decapitated man. At least the blood has stopped pooling. Still, she tries to shift away and fails.

"Yes."

"Who are they to you?"

"It doesn't matter. Do we have a deal?"

"Are they yours?"

How old does she think I am? I would have been fifteen years old when Saad was born. "No."

"Then why—?"

"Do we have a deal?" I evade the question. It's none of her business. She doesn't need to know anything personal about me.

"Tell me who they are," she pushes. "You know how much I care about my mother. You know where I live. You know the worst of my actions. Let me at least know who they are, if you want me to protect them."

She puts forward a good argument, but . . . "You are not in the position to bargain, Sariq."

I could almost swear she nearly smiled when I called her that. She takes a moment to consider. "Fine, I'll protect them if you don't make it back."

"Good. And I'll make sure you make it back. Inshallah." That means by the will of God.

"Ameen." She manages to pull her knees up to her chest, but still can't manage to move her arms.

"Alright, come on." I lift her up into my arms so that her legs dangle to my right. She sighs, her head tilting to lean against my chest. "Akilah will kill me if we take a second longer."

We step out into the light, the fresh air replacing the smell of flesh and blood.

She breathes in the smell of me. The sensation of her breath against my neck nearly makes me shiver. "Zayen," she draws out my name like it's a delicacy she'd like to devour.

"Yeah?" When she doesn't respond, I look down at her. Her eyes are fluttering closed, her body seeming to relax into mine. The act of trust makes me feel more protective over her, wishing there was more I could do to help ease her pain. "Are you okay?"

She takes a deep breath. "Hmm." The sound is barely audible. It softens my heart for the slightest moment, reminding me of how I felt when I'd sneak out to see Saad and Aya.

Every time I'd see them waiting in that outside room, excitement in their eyes as soon as I'd step in—and I left them. Alone and confused, I left them, without any explanation.

The pain settles back in place, making me wish I could be as numb as the thief is now.

"About time," Nawaz riles, getting to his feet. It's funny how he has gone from palaces to sleeping on thin mats and waiting around on dirt floors. He takes note of the way I am carrying the thief. "Is she okay?"

I almost drop her with exhaustion. "She will be." No thanks to you, prince.

"Do you want me to take her from you?" I know his words are shaped into a purposeful weapon. The real meaning behind his question is just a reminder of his undeserved power.

If I say no, if I react at all, it will only add fuel to his fire. He steps up to me and I drop her into his arms—silently grateful for the break.

"Pathetic." Akilah shakes her head, lifting a bag over her shoulder and walking further into the man-made hole in the mountain.

"Where are we going?" I ask, following Akilah blindly.

The vibration of my voice makes the thief stir. Her eyes flutter open. As soon as she sees Nawaz, she reaches out for him like a child.

Anger burns in my throat at the action. After I help her—after I carry her to safety when she needed me—she still reaches for him.

He smirks like he won at some sort of non-existent competition.

"Alara," he says her true name for what might be the first time. He says it gently. "Hi, beautiful."

And there it is again—those flashes of memories. The way he touched the woman I loved, holding her face like he actually wanted her. But truly he just wanted to hurt me.

And I don't know why.

But whatever he is trying now won't bother me. He can do whatever he wants, as he always has.

He holds her close, and she smiles sleepily. Her head settles against his chest. I hope he smells bad. I'm supposed to not let it bother me, but why the hell does she trust him more than me?

Nawaz meets my gaze, and must notice my frustration because something light sparks in his eyes as he walks beside me.

The corners of his lips turn up. It makes me want to use the twenty-something years of training I have received on him.

The path we follow under the hill soon becomes pitch black, and I slow my pace to increase the awareness of my surroundings. There are only the footsteps of three people—a good start.

I trail the pads of my fingers along the side of the wall. It seems to be man made, just like the mountain that we went through.

It had strange writing on the ceiling. Akilah hadn't even glanced at it when I pointed it out, and when I was trying to figure out what it meant, she claimed that we don't have time and didn't look back.

Almost like she knew.

Are there engravings on this passage too? Things that we wouldn't understand, but she does. Where is it taking us?

"Akilah?" I call out.

Silence follows.

I reach out, following the sounds of the footsteps. Heavier steps come from beside me, which I know are Nawaz's.

Rushing forward, I grab ahold of a body and slam them down against the floor. I punch them in the jaw and they grunt—giving away that it is a man and not Akilah.

I punch again and again until their will to fight stops. They block their face. "Tawaqaf ean darbi!" He shouts at me to stop hitting him.

"Who are you?" I growl. I straddle his chest and keep his arms pinned down to the ground. "Where is Akilah?"

"Who? I-I don't know! I've been—"

The sound of other footsteps running in our direction makes me rise to my feet. I go to block their path from Nawaz and the thief.

From the amount of footsteps coming towards towards us, I already know I have broken my promise to myself. I won't win this fight. It's in the dark and we are outnumbered.

I unsheathe the sword on my back and hold it in front of me. If I'm going down, I'm going to take at least two or three of them with me.

As soon as I hear footsteps close enough, I curve my sword up and slash it downwards.

A man cries out in pain and I hear his body thump as he hits the ground. I'm not sure if he is dead, but it is good enough for me.

The next man comes unexpectedly, his footsteps light. I feel the brush of air in the speed of his moments and use that to follow him. Again, my weapon cuts through the air and knocks him down.

Footsteps seem to come in all directions—too many to count.

I told the thief not to get captured, yet here I am with no choice. It's funny how life throws lessons in my face like this, to show that everything is circumstantial. There is no avoiding this.

It is the perfect set up. I knew I couldn't trust Akilah, but for her to do this wasn't expected.

Hands grab me and shove me to the ground. The shock of impact goes through my body, and I feel it in my teeth. I want to see Nawaz and the thief, but I can't. I failed to protect both of them.

"Nawaz," I rasp.

"Yeah?"

"Is she okay?" There is a ringing in my ears.

"Are any of us?"

"Are any of us?"

CHAPTER 21

Alara: I need a break.

Just a single moment of escape where I'm not doing, or thinking, or fighting. To be able to breathe again, in a way I haven't in a long time.

Funny that I ask for a moment, while being trapped in a cage. Alone. I don't know what happened. One moment I'm falling asleep in Zayen's arms and the next I'm in a dark cell with nobody around.

I tried calling out—but I'm not sure if that was a good idea. What if another giant man comes to hurt me? What if worse comes? But I had to know if Zayen or Akilah or Nawaz are here.

There was no response.

At least I'm not in chains and my arms won't go numb. My body still aches from the hits that I took from that man-creature

I see now that when faced with impossibly messed up, inescapable and life-threatening situations, it is better to see the positive.

And not being in chains is just about the only thing I can think of.

In the damp coldness, I rise to my feet. My body aches with a tiredness that surpasses lack of sleep. My limbs are mostly numb as I walk across the five steps to the bars of the cage.

I really just want to bathe. It makes me miss the pathetic, cracked bucket that my mom and I used to dip cloths in to wipe ourselves with.

"Hello?" I call again, louder this time.

I can't stand being in here. Let the monsters come. I just need something to happen, to understand what situation I am in. For all I know, I could be waiting to be eaten by cannibals.

With the situations I have found myself in lately, I would not be that surprised.

A low growl, the sound like a tortured animal, vibrates through the dark empty hall in front of my cell.

"Who's there?" they ask, their voice rough and deep.

The sound unwillingly sends shivers through me. And then a rush of relief. "Zayen?"

"Sariq?"

I almost laugh. He's here. Maybe he will have answers that will fill in the gaps. "W-What is going on?"

An empty silence follows my question. Did he pass out or something? "I'm sorry," he finally says.

"Sorry? Did—Where are we? Are you okay?" He doesn't sound okay.

"I messed up. I'm sorry."

"You did this?"

"Well, technically no. I think Akilah did—"

"Akilah?" I knew it. With every step I took, I knew it and still I did nothing. What was I supposed to do? Call her out? Tell the prince? Tell the Hakeem? No ways.

I had to hope for the best. Which didn't work out in my favour, clearly. "Do you know where we are?" I ask.

"We were ambushed. I don't know who they are or what they want. Made us walk for hours and placed bags over our head to make sure we saw nothing—so in terms of where we are or what will happen, I have no idea."

My fingers wrap around the cold, oxidised bars that cage me in. I try to lean my head against my hands and look down the hallways for any other signs of life, but there are none.

"Hey, uh . . ." I don't want to say his name, in case. "Dude."

He chuckles. "Am I 'dude'?"

"You think anyone else is in here with us?" Listening.

"Probably. And I don't know where Nawaz is. I haven't seen him."

Oh, we are so screwed. My knees suddenly feel like jelly and I slide down to the floor, my heart caving in on itself.

The reason the stupid Hakeem even sent us on this stupid journey was to protect his stupid son. Now, my mother . . . Will I get to see her again? What if I don't get a chance to hug her?

"We can't assume he is dead," Zayen adds in, most likely knowing that I am having the same thoughts he would be. He must really love them. "Not many people would have the guts to do it, because it would mean war."

"This is your fault," I huff. I just want to be angry at someone. There is nobody else to direct this feeling to. and if I don't release it I will go crazy. I may just start banging my fists against the dark grey walls of my confines.

He is an easy target.

"At least I wasn't asleep the entire time," he grumbles. "If a war were to happen, I bet you'd sleep through it."

"If a war were to happen I bet you'd lose it." He's silent for longer than I expected. I thought he'd feel as frustrated as I do. I wouldn't mind being an outlet for him. Yet he doesn't insult me back. "I'm sorry."

"It's fine." His voice is deep and rough. It cuts through the air like a serrated knife.

I almost wish I was in his cell. All I want is to be hugged. I want is his big arms wrapped around me and that spicy oud that he wears to calm my senses. To help me feel like I will be okay.

I don't trust him, but I don't care. In a world like this, I can't trust anyone, but I need to be hugged. Just for a second.

Footsteps shuffle somewhere close by, followed by the soft jungle of keys. I immediately get to my feet and move into the darkest part of my cell, preparing to fight.

A gate swings open and a commotion sounds nearby. I want to call Zayen's name, to know that he is okay, but it feels as if I have swallowed cotton and it is stuck in my throat.

Barely able to breathe, I squeeze my fists together and hold them out in front of me. I can gather everything I have been feeling and take it out on the unlucky person who gets close to me.

A guard comes to my gate, barely even looking in my direction as he pushes the key into the lock.

One.

The gate whines as it swings, sounding like a child's high pitched cries.

Two.

The guard steps in. His body is covered from head to toe and he wears the checkered black and white keffiyeh on his head that Zayen has been wearing—the one he took when he got into that fight.

Three.

I jump forward, my fist coming into contact with his jaw. His head is thrown back. He grunts. The millisecond that I take, not knowing what move to make next, is a mistake.

He recovers instantly and grabs me. A sound of protest leaves my lips as I try to force myself away from the man, but there are more guards surrounding us already.

A black bag covers my head. It smells like chai spices. My body continues to wriggle until my feet are lifted up off the ground and I am carried out.

"Dude!" I call, hoping Zayen knows I'm referring to him. I don't want to give away his name. Any information could be dangerous in the hands of the wrong person.

"Fight!" he calls back, grunting. The sound of his voice is followed by a loud thump, that I hope was his fists against the guard's beloved body parts.

I kick out with my legs, knocking it into the knee of the man carrying me. Not giving him a second to recover, I kick a second and third time until his grip loosens.

My hand flies up to pull off the black bag covering my head and I find two more guards coming towards me. I panic, not knowing how to fight one man let alone two.

The one comes towards me and tries to get ahold of me, and I swing my fist up, hoping for the best. The guard doesn't try to injure me back, even as rage fills his eyes. Strange.

Someone grabs me from the back and I use every edge and hard part of my body, from my elbows to my feet, to fight back. My lack of experience is clear when I can't get out again, and they position themselves so I can't do much damage.

My head turns, looking for Zayen. His eyes land on me as he ducks away from another guard and sweeps his feet down in a rotation that takes the guard off balance. His training is has made each movement precise and I can't do anything but stare as he lands each hit like it is an art.

The guard holding me starts leading me away, realising that standing around is only going to get him injured.

I push myself forward but his grip on my upper arms is so tight that it begins to ache. "Stop." Fear trickles into my body. I try to use my previous tactic of flailing my body parts around, but it doesn't work this time.

As my body straightens, I find Zayen in front of me. Goose-bumps rise on my skin. He is looking at the guard with a deep rage. An animalistic growl leaves his throat.

Before, I thought that he hated me as much as I hated him. But seeing the look in his eyes now . . . This is as if every deep, angry emotion has crawled to the surface.

Let her go.

CHAPTER 22

Z ayen: The guard that was holding Alara took one look around the room and dashed out. I shouldn't have let him go—because it's likely he will come back with more guards.

My fists are already going numb and I don't know how many more I can take on.

"Why do you look so . . ." Alara's eyes travel over my face and body. "Like you're going to destroy everything that gets close to you."

Because I am. Because the anger that is burning inside me is nearly blinding.

I promised to protect Alara and I couldn't. Seeing her in that guards hands, being handled like a doll made me—

And Nawaz is nowhere to be seen. He could be dead or being tortured for information.

And without him, I lose those kids. If Alara and I get out of here safely, it won't matter, because the only two people I live for would be gone.

I step forward and hold onto Alara. She lets me. "Are you okay?" I ask. It's a stupid question, with everything that is going on, but I need to know.

She nods, her eyes wide with surprise and something else. "Thank you."

Hearing those words from her lips hits all the right spots of my ego. The corner of my lip lifts. If we were friends, if the situation was different, I might have leaned down and kissed her.

She shifts closer, her eyes dropping to my lips for barely a second. Oh, how I really wish the situation was different.

My grip on her tightens as my body fights my mind. "We—" My voice comes out rough and breathless. "We should get out of here. Should we look for Nawaz?"

"Yeah, we have to." Unfortunately.

She hesitantly steps back, her arms wrapping around herself. "I really need to learn how to fight. I'm sorry."

"You did well. Using your body as a weapon is a great start." Her smile is slow and shy. She tries to turn away to hide it from me. "Are you blushing?" I tease.

Her smile falls and she meets my gaze again. There's a fierce defiance in her eyes, like she'd rather be doing absolutely anything other than hearing my compliments. "We have to go."

I step closer, the back of my hand brushing against her cheek. Even in the dim lighting of this prison-style hallway, I see the look in her eyes shift from fear to confusion to . . . something.

Stop. My hand slowly slides down her arm. She doesn't move, allowing me to reach all the way to her hand. My fingers linger over hers for a moment before I drop my hand to my side.

"Why did you let me do that?" I ask. She should have stepped away, should have done something.

"Why did you do it?" she retorts.

Because of that look in her eyes. Because my ego is hurt after all of the fights I have lost, but when I feel the softness of her skin beneath my touch it reminds me that there are other ways to win, besides fighting. "I . . . I don't know."

She nods and takes a step towards the exit, but I stop her.

"We should try going that way." I nod my chin down the passage, in the opposite direction of where she wants to go. "In the opposite direction of where all the guards came from, yeah?"

Her face scrunches and I can see she knows it's a better idea. She won't admit it though.

I start walking and know she'll follow. Although there's no way to know what we are walking towards, or if there is any way out of this mess.

My footsteps echo and I don't dare to look anywhere but forward. There are cages that line the right side of the wall and I don't want to see who is trapped inside or what they look like.

This passage is endless and seems to curve around whatever building we are in.

"There," Alara whispers, breaking the haunting silence. She rushes forward to a heavy wooden door, but I grab her arm.

She jerks back and her head whips to me, frowning. "What are you doing?"

"Let me go first, to be safe." I did promise to protect her, although I'm not doing a great job of it based on the situation.

The door has a black, metallic knob that is frozen to the touch. I twist it and it takes a lot of force before it caves and opens, the sound indicating that it has not been used in a long time. A good sign for us.

It opens to stairway that, four steps in, becomes pitch black. It has a dry, dusty smell.

I reach my arm back and open my palm. The thief understands and slips her fingers into mine.

The journey down is tedious. With every step, I remember Saad and Aya. Their innocent smiles, the way the would wait in the darkness until I arrived. They were always so good, so patient, and they deserve so much better.

I wanted to give them a life better than the one that was served to them. But now . . . My heart squeezes in my chest until it's hard to breathe, not only because of the lack of fresh air around us.

The stairs come to an end and light outlines the shape of a door. Alara's hand quickly slips out of mine when I stop.

I take two deep breaths. Whatever happens once we cross that door is going to change everything. Because we're going in blind, against an unknown number of people, and we have nothing to offer or negotiate with.

"Stay behind me," I say, my throat dry with unease.

"Zayen."

I turn to her. I can hear the fear in her voice. The question—will we survive this?

"You're going to be okay, Sariq." It's dark, but I can see her silhouette and the soft curls brushed back behind her ears.

Her hand lifts to my cheek. Her touch is gentle and warm. I lean into it, my gaze falling closed for a moment. It gives me a strange feeling of stillness.

I haven't felt this way since . . .

The thought nearly makes me pull away, until her other hand comes to my left cheek. She leans up on her toes.

I smile, biting my lip. She's too short to reach my face.

Kneeling down, I slip my hands behind her thighs and lift her up, pulling her against me.

A soft gasp leaves her lips. Her legs close around me, her arms wrapping behind my neck. She has probably never done anything like this before.

Energy fills me, making my pulse race. I press her back against the wall beside the door, my head lowering to her neck. She dips her head to the side, giving herself to me.

It makes me breathless for a moment—and then I get to work trying to make her just as breathless. It works fast. Soft, un-contained moans leave her lips, her legs wrap tighter around me. "Please," she whispers. Damn.

I want to give her everything.

I want to make her toes curl. I pause for a moment, needing to catch my breath, but she starts placing kisses against my jaw until she is at the corner of my mouth.

Her lips align with mine but she doesn't kiss me. Her chest presses against mine every time she inhales. She waits for me to move in, and I can't stop myself. I have to kiss her. She's mine.

I pull back, the fear and shock over that thought creating an uncomfortable pressure in my chest.

I can't be thinking that. Not now, and not with the game that Nawaz had been playing with her. If I kiss her I will definitely become possessive of her. I can't allow that. There is too much at risk.

"We should go," I say, lowering her back to the ground.

"But—"

"Nawaz could be dead. We need to go."

A hard wall of defiance closes around my chest, leaving me feeling frustrated and angry. The perfect emotions for what we are about to walk into.

I twist the handle and it barely budges. Worry slices through me, that I wasted our time by coming this route. Twisting again, it budges a bit more. It clearly hasn't been used in a long time.

On the third try, it twists enough that the door clicks open. Light floods in. I resist the urge to look back at Alara, to find out if her cheeks are tinted red. I wonder if her eyes would trail to my lips at the idea of what might have happened.

There is a brightly lit hallway. It's white walls contain blue, delicately painted patterns that swirl and sway like depictions of the ocean and everything it contains. It's beautiful and the exact opposite to the cages we woke up in.

"How are we going to him them? This place is hu—" I press my index finger to her lips. They're so soft that I nearly push her back into the darkness to finish what we had started.

Her voice was echoing off the walls. I had to shut her up. Shaking my head, I say, "Shh. We'll find him." We don't have any other choice.

She finally looks around. Her eyes shine in the light streaming through the tall windows that line the right side of the wall. "This place is . . ." She frowns. "What is it?"

"I don't know, but it's bigger than the palace which means that they're not nobody."

"Great," she huffs under her breath, stalking forward

I told her to stay behind me.

Alara freezes when two guards run past the archway at the other end of the hall. She glances back at me and then launches into a sprint.

I follow after her, keeping my feet light to avoid any unnecessary extra noise. When we reach the archway, we curve in the direction that the guards ran and stop.

Okay, to be fair we were making bad decisions and this was likely to happen.

There is only one door on this side of the passageway, and it is guarded by six or seven guards. From what I can assume, there are more guards inside and putting up a fight will only get us in more trouble.

Three guards rush towards us and seize us. I grunt as one roughly grabs my arms and pushes me forward, towards the room. It's not that it is painful, but it's just frustrating to constantly feel like I am losing.

The gigantic room that we are pushed into makes me forget about everything else. It's not like anything I've seen before, even as a guard for the royal family.

The walls of the unbelievably beautiful room are made of a deep blue tinted glass. The glass undulates and curves so that with each movement, the lights from the intricate lanterns dance over the walls the way the light of the sun would dance over the waves of the ocean.

At the other end of the room, there is a golden throne and beside it is a plain wooden chair.

And in that chair, Nawaz sits.

CHAPTER 23

Alara: Nawaz.

He looks like he is possessed. His head is tilted up. Sweat beads his brows and his eyes are nearly rolling into the back of his head. Short, pained gasps come from him.

Zayen instinctively steps forward but the two guards behind him keep him in place. He is bigger than both of them.

"Lovely for you to finally join us," says a deep, kind voice. He's got light, sagging skin and a stark white beard that matches his hair. It contrasts the dark brown of his eyes.

The kindness in his voice immediately puts me on edge, reminding me of how the Hakeem smiled and acted kind as long as it was for his gain.

Until he trapped my mother and sent me on a death mission.

"Let him go. You're making a mistake. If you harm him, there's going to be a war!"

"Harm him?" The man chuckles. His laugh is hoarse. "I won't harm him. I am simply asking him a few questions."

"Making him unconscious." Zayn gestures with his hand to Nawaz's dazed look. "Is harm."

"And you're suddenly the caring older brother, I see."

His statement leaves a deafening silence in the room. Zayen stills, like a cat that turned a corner and found the most vicious looking dog.

Older brother? The way Zayen is acting . . .

But that would mean that Zayen is royalty, so why would be be working as a guard? I know the Hakeem isn't very nice, but to treat his own sun that badly doesn't seem likely. Surely.

If he has a strong, capable son, why would the Hakeem hide that? And there is no way that nobody knows that he exists. This land of Ahlam watches their ruler, and would know if there was more than one prince. We would have seen it posted on the news boards.

Zayen.

A prince.

No, it's not possible. My mind spins and it makes me nauseous. "Zayen?" I ask. I need to know if it is true, to stop the mess that is being built in my mind.

His head turns to me slowly, as if he momentarily forgot that I existed. He's eyes are pained. There's something dark and unknown swirling in them. It creases the sides of his eyes with pain and disappointment.

The look alone tells me that what is being claimed is true.

Oh. My heart jumps into my throat.

Slowly, his eyes turn back to the man. "You're lying."

He sighs, as if he had expected this reaction from Zayen. His expression looks like he is not enjoying the pain on Zayen's face. Usually evil people enjoying seeing pain, don't they?

"It is a grave sin to lie. You and I both know what comes out of my mouth is not a lie."

Zayen tries again to jerk forward, out of the grasp of the guard. A low groan leaves his lips. It reminds me of a beast trying to escape its shackles.

It's as if Zayen knows this information but does not want to hear it out loud—as if in silence the truth is not real.

"Your brother knows," the man says. "He confirmed it." The man turns his head to Nawaz, who stares blindly at the ceiling. "Tell them what you know, prince."

Nawaz's eyes suddenly shift to us. His voice is monotonous when he says, "I found a letter that our father wrote. He wrote it to your mother, explaining that he agreed not to kill you but that you will never be royalty. It said that you knew about who you are. That made me angry because we always used to play together. I thought we were friends." His voice lowers, emotion filling his voice. "But you're a liar. You knew and you never told me. If you don't want to be my brother then I'll never treat you like one."

Has Nawaz treated Zayen badly? What did he do?

I turn to Zayen and he seems to be breaking from the inside out. His breathe shakes and he lowers his gaze to the floor, almost ashamed to hear his brother's admission.

Zayen's voice is strained when he says, "I wanted to tell you. I just didn't know how. I always said 'one day', but it never came.

We never get back our yesterdays and our tomorrows never come. I'm sorry that I never gave you the truth."

"You're not forgiven."

"Enough," the man says and Nawaz's gaze seems to lazily drift back up to the ceiling. What has he done to Nawaz? "Do you still claim that I am lying?"

Zayen's body relaxes, and he stops trying to fight out of the grip of the guards. Then, like lightening that comes during a sunny day, he shifts his body and elbows one guard. They jerk back and the other comes for him, but he is too quick and has the guard on the floor before I can blink.

He gets away from the guards and reaches the man on the throne. "Tell me what you want."

"Or what?" The man does not seem bothered in the slightest at Zayen's fighting skills. "Will you try to knock me onto the ground, too? Then what? You'll take an unconscious prince through a building full of guards ready to arrest you. Either go stand back in your place, or I can have you placed back in your cages until you're ready to play nice."

I don't want to go back in there.

I can't see Zayen's face. I'm sure he is thinking of all the ways he can decapitate this man. He finally swivels on his feet and comes to stand back at my side.

Two guards step up to get ahold of him again, but he puts his hand up. "I am not going to run, but if you touch me I will hurt you."

I shift to turn back and look at the one guard holding me, and he smiles at me. This is so weird. I don't think I've seen any of the guards at the royal palace smile at me—even when they thought I was royalty. Not even Zayen smiled.

"Who are you?" I ask.

His eyes find mine and watch me for a long time, like he is taking in and memorising every feature. "Who are you? Why are you traveling with royalty?"

"It's a long story."

"It always is." He turns his head and gestures with a single finger to someone behind us. "And you will have all of your questions answered, and doubts resolved. But for now I want you to go and get cleaned up. I will have my guards show you to your quarters. Don't do anything stupid and your safety will remain intact."

The guards holding us lead us out of the large ballroom-sized room. My heart seems to find it's way into my throat and I turn to look at Zayen. He is staring straight ahead, his expression hard and cold.

I want him to look at me, to tell me it'll be okay. I want him to hold my hand or wrap his arms around me again. But he's a thousand miles away, lost in his own mind.

They lead us across the passageway and across, to a plain white while that rises up tall. One guard pushes against the hard white surface and it budges open.

I should have known! Stupid giant buildings and their stupid secret doors.

The guard still holding onto my wrist leads me forward, into an oval-shaped atrium. It's brightly lit, with the entire ceiling made of glass, allowing for the clear blue skies to peak in on us.

I stare up at the clouds that dance above us. The last time I'd seen the sky was when Zayen was carrying me out of that cave that I had been chained in.

The memory is so strange and surreal. Every moment since I went to that harbour market in my home town of Wadi feels like it has been a strange fever dream.

I keep placing one foot in front of the other, telling myself that it'll turn out okay, but what if it doesn't?

The guards lead us further down one of the passages that branch out from the atrium. I look over at Zayen again, wishing he'd look at me. They're probably going to lock us in those cages again, and I won't get to see those soft brown eyes again.

They remind me of what it feels like to step onto soil without shoes and smell the fresh earth around me.

I want him to look at me. Just once. Just for a second.

The passageway is white—it seems like there is a consistent theme of marine life and strange creatures that inspired this building. Paintings of waves and strange writings lines the walls.

We pass wooden doors that repeat themselves every few feet. On the other side of the walls are windows that are blocked by sheer white curtains. The guard leading me suddenly comes to a halt, jerking me back. For a moment, I think the worst—that there is some trap waiting for me. That I am alone with a bunch of men I know nothing about and I have no skills in fighting.

The feeling of vulnerability makes me want to cave into myself. I glance over at Zayen again, and he is looking at me.

I feel caught, as if he can sense the emotions I am feeling. He finally looked, and suddenly I wish he didn't.

He tilts his head in a slight nod. "You okay, dude?"

A short laugh leaves my lips. I had expected him to use 'sariq'. "All good, dude."

The corners of his mouth lifts. My gaze shifts to the floor out of fear of my thoughts. That maybe, with the perfect lighting in these hallways, he looks . . . breathtakingly handsome.

It was a lot easier to almost kiss him, when we were in a dark stairway. Now I have to remember that he is, in fact, a prince.

That thought alone brings the unease back tenfold. I have so many questions, and I doubt I will get the answer to any of them.

Is he older than Nawaz? Is he the true heir? Why would his father do that? My mind spins as I am lead into a oval-shaped room.

The walls are made of a smooth white paint. On the walls hang gold-framed images of nature. The floor is made of a dark brown wood. A pristine white bed sits against an engraved alcove. If I thought that the room I was given in the royal palace in Quadura was fancy, I clearly had no idea.

Not that I had a chance to sleep in that bed.

I turn to the guards. "I sleep here?" The guard who had been leading me nods. "Alone?" My gaze goes to Zayen.

He steps toward me, almost protectively. "No. You're not going to be alone in here. The last time I left you alone in a bedroom you ended up taking a solo tour and getting thrown in prison."

"Rules do not permit men to sleep alone with an unwed woman. You will have your own private bedroom next door."

His gaze is fierce. "No, I am not leaving her. We don't have to be alone. There can be another guard. But I am staying here." He points to the light brown couch in the corner. "I'll sleep there."

Zayen wants to stay with me.

That brings me relief. With the strange power that this unknown man has over Nawaz, I do not want to find myself being taken in my sleep and put into the same trance.

The guards all look at each other, unsure on whether they should push the issue. Eventually, one tall, lanky guard nods. "I will remain outside. The door will stay open."

Thank you.

CHAPTER 24

Zayen: Alara and I stand in the same hall where Nawaz admitted that he knew he was my brother.

There was nothing to say to him—especially because he was under a trance and would most likely not hear a thing.

But this whole time, he knew. When he had his personal guards beat me, he knew he was doing it to his brother. When he stood beside our father at royal dinners, he knew I should be standing with them too.

He was angry. Because I hid the truth.

I failed to be a brother. And I feel like I have failed again. Now, this unknown man has power over the prince. Not only that, but he could have power over me as well because the knowledge of me being the true heir could be detrimental.

Alara brushes her fingers through her curls nervously. She has on a new white Abaya, made of silk. I wear the matching thobe. Her eyes find mine and she shares a small smile with me. "Thank you for staying with me all night."

As if I would let her out of my sight. I told her I will protect her.

There were many times through the night where I wanted nothing more than to climb into bed with her and pull her into my body. She made the most adorable sounds in her sleep. But we followed the guidelines given.

I stayed far away from her, with the door open. It made me miss my best friend, Ali. He would have laughed at me for being such a rule follower. He would always do everything he is not supposed to, and would somehow get away with it.

I wonder how he is now. If he is still the same. Everything happened so fast that I never got to see him before we left.

My hand lifts to touch Alara, wanting to feel the softness of her skin. I quickly drop it, realising that would be stupid and inappropriate. Sometimes things happen so fast. We can lose people we care about in an instant. Right now, she is the only sense of familiarity I have.

Maybe that is why we nearly kissed in the dark. It was on my mind all night. I couldn't figure out why I would want to do that with her, but I think it was only because I was trying to keep her close. I'm glad we didn't go through with it. We can't mess this up.

The man who seized us walks in. He wears a plain white thobe, identical to mine. Akilah walks in beside him, her chin held high.

My jaw clenches. There are so many things I want to do to harm her. She looks over at Alara and I and sighs deeply. "Oh, don't look at me like that." Her navy black hair is tied into a long, perfectly neat ponytail. "You two both knew you were taking a major risk by following me. I had nothing to lose, and you did. Simply put, you made a bad choice."

"But," adds the older man. Everything about him is neat—from the lining of his beard to his spotless shoes. "We do not want you to lose."

That doesn't seem true.

"Right," Alara says under her breath.

He steps towards her. "You must take accountability. You made the choice to follow a stranger in a world based on dominance. The world is always at war, always fighting against or for something, and you can not follow blindly. You have to look at the facts, which you did not."

That silences Alara, because it's true. We followed with emotion clouding our vision. With our loved ones at risk and no real factual evidence to go by.

Maybe my ability to fight well is less about combat, and more about making the right choices.

"I want you to dine with me," he says, gesturing towards a wooden door to the right of us. "Then we can have a tasteful discussion over a delicious meal."

He could easily poison us. But then again, there are much easier ways to kill us considering that we both fell asleep in his home.

He has a very powerful presence. I've been around the Hakeem my whole life and have never felt it.

With the Hakeem everything always felt like it was for show—the guards, the pretty gardens, the huge events. He wanted power and privilege.

What does this man want?

That question is the only reason I turn and lead myself towards the door.

A guard stands outside. He holds his arm out, blocking me from passing. "Shoes," is all he says.

"Apologies, but it is a tradition. Plus, I have white rugs that I'd like to keep white," the old man says.

I turn to him, keeping my posture tall. I'm possibly a head taller than him. I can be scary. Maybe that's why my father let me be a guard, when he could have hid me as a servant. "I'd like to know your name before I get comfortable in your home," I insist. I can't keep referring to him as an old man.

"I am the Wazir of this land. You may call me by my name, Ameer." The Wazir. Surely not. "I'm sure that brings up more questions, which is why I suggested we dine." He gestures with one hand to the room. His hands are wrinkled with age and contain deep blue veins that run up his arms.

Both Alara and I remove our shoes, leaving them outside. I'm very glad I have socks on, and that the old m—the Wazir allowed us to bathe and change.

The room is beautiful. White rugs line the floor, contrasting the brown table at its centre. Lush white pillows with gold stitching and patterns are placed around the table. Gold plates and vases are set on the table, with white roses as decorations.

It's similar to the palace in Qadura in design, yet completely different. Everything feels foreign here.

"We eat here?" Alara asks, her cheeks flushed.

I nearly smile. The memories of her home come back, of the mat she used as a bed and the broken bucket she used to clean herself with.

It is unimaginable to know people live like that, but to her it must be unimaginable that people live like this.

We all lower ourselves onto the cushions, including Akilah. I watch her closely.

"So—"

Alara cuts off Ameer. "Where is Nawaz? Why is he not here?"

I almost feel guilty for not having thought of Nawaz. I was too busy wanting to know about where we are and how this man could be the Wazir.

"Let me ask you a question first," he says.

Another man, also in all white clothing, places a basket of breads down on the table.

"Can you define goodness to me. What does it mean to be a good person?"

Alara frowns. She folds her arms on her lap and under the table, she nervously fiddles with her fingers. "To always do the right thing."

"Sure, that's given." He tilts his head. "But what is the right thing?"

A fist bangs against the table, causing it to rattle. "Amana." Honesty. "But we're in a room full of liars, no?"

CHAPTER 25

Alara: Akilah looks around the room, her eyes reflecting the fires that light the room. The lines between her eyebrows are creased with concern.

"Oh, how rich of you to call anyone else a liar." Zayen can be scary when he is angry. I haven't seen him like this since the Hakeem—his father—threatened to harm those kids. "You're a traitor. You swore an oath."

The anger in his eyes match the ferocity of Akilah's. His hands ball into fists at his sides. I wonder what he would be doing to her, if there weren't other people around.

My fingers squeeze together, my body fighting the urge to run. I'm so tired of conflict. I have grown up on the run. That's what I have always done, in order avoid conflict and never be caught. This—all of the emotions and fighting—it is abnormal.

I don't know what to do with it. I don't know how to escape it.

It's a strange feeling, to miss the life I tried to get escape from.

Every day I fought for more. I stole for more. I took care of my mother, so we could have more.

Now I am here. My mother, technically, is living in a palace. I have food on my plate. I have a bed to sleep in. I have adventure and challenge, something different.

And yet every part of me wants to run.

A large hand slides over my own. Their skin is warm. I immediately pull my hand away, feeling disoriented. The world comes back into focus and I look at the hand that is now on my lap, my heart racing.

Zayen.

My breath hitches, going half way up my throat and then stopping completely.

He shares a small smile with me, curving up the corners of his lips. My eyes remain on that curve for a moment. "You okay?"

I nod quickly. "Yeah, sorry." My gaze goes to Akilah and Ameer. They're both watching us.

Zayen slides his hand away. His knee stays pressed against mine as we sit. My heart jumps inside my chest like a kid that ate too much candy. I nearly reach out to hold it again. His touch is comforting. I want it back.

"Back to my question. A good person. What does that look like to you?"

"Someone with values. Generosity. Caring for others. What Akilah said, honesty." She meets my gaze and lifts an eyebrow. The look makes me feel like she is accusing me of something.

I raise my eyebrow back at her. What?

"Do you see what those values have in common?" he asks me.

That they're good? I shrug. I don't want to say something stupid. I've never been asked these kinds of questions.

At school, we were taught to read and speak. After that, they leave us to homeschool to make space for incoming students. But my mom was always too sad, too holed up in her own mind, to home-school me.

But I turned out fine, I guess.

The old man, Ameer, then looks at Zayen. "Tell me what you think."

Zayen tilts his head. "That they're all benefitting other people instead of ourselves." How could I not have realised such an obvious thing?

I wonder if he was trained and tutored with Nawaz. Or if they had lessons for the guards in the palace. Or maybe he learnt in secret, taking books from that gigantic library with the three doors, when nobody was looking.

I wonder if he can teach me more about the world. I wonder if those lips could teach me what it feels like to kiss.

I turn to look at him again, at his side profile. The curve of his cheekbones. The arch of his eyebrows. His tanned skin. The beard that lines his jaw neatly—he must have shaven when he showered.

There are two beauty spots on the back, left side of his neck that I'd never noticed before. I wonder if he would shiver if I traced my fingers between them, like I'm connecting a constellation. I wonder if he has any more.

The feeling of his leg against mine suddenly makes me nervous. Is it something he notices, that we are touching? Is he sitting closer to me on purpose?

"Exactly. Isn't that our purpose of being here? We get the most, feel the happiest, when we're creating bonds and giving to others."

I quickly look away before anyone can catch me staring. I should be focusing on getting information. Or at least focusing on the discussion.

I shift forward so his leg is no longer touching mine. "Isn't there more to our purpose? You know, because what about people who have nothing to give?"

I've always felt like people would laugh at me. In school, I was always afraid of that. But I think silence would be worse.

I don't know what kind of answer I'll get, but the best way to learn is to ask.

He smiles at that question. "I want you to leave my home tonight."

That makes my heart jump like a firework, for a completely different reason than Zayen's touch. Did I ask the wrong question? Did I offend him? Where are we going to stay?

"Go out. See for yourself. Find your answers and come back to tell me what you learn."

"Go out?" I parrot.

I don't know what's waiting out there for us. I've never heard much about Diyar.

Ardifa is the 'haunted' forests where all the stories are created. The stories of monsters and darkness. The stories that are made to tell around fires or to tell kids at bedtime. But Diyar . . . Nothing. Nobody ever speaks about Diyar.

That scares me much more.

CHAPTER 26

Zayen: This time I didn't forget Nawaz.

Ameer, the Wazir, tried to convince us not to see Nawaz, but after everything it was needed. He was asleep—something that is 'normal' after his brain was hijacked.

There are many things that can go wrong because of us leaving Nawaz with the Wazir—but there is already a mile-high pile of things that have gone wrong.

And it is killing me inside, because each wrong step means I am putting Saad and Aya in danger. And each step away from Nawaz, into this new city, feels wrong.

The sun is half way down the horizon, leaving the skies a mess of peaches and pinks.

The roads are busy, each passageway lined with vendors selling fresh falafels and juiced fruits.

The people here are dressed differently—none of them wear any finery. There is no way to tell if they are rich or poor, as they all have decent and clean clothing.

Even though everywhere I look, there are people, none of them are shouting or trying to sell their products by shoving it in peoples faces—which is the only way people sold things in the souks of Qadura.

It's peaceful.

My breath is sucked out of my lungs. "Do you see that?" I ask Alara, but I am walking towards it before I can hear her respond.

A lantern. No, not a lantern. Lanterns use fire. This ... There's a blue light that seems to continuously shift inside the lantern container.

I reach out to lift it, to see if there is some strange trick, but there is no way to fake something like this. It is another form of light.

"Would you like to trade? It is a specialty, directly from Aleamiq," the man in the stall says. From Aleamiq? The prison?

How does the Hakeem not know about the existence of this? It is probably more priceless than anything he's ever touched, and if he knew it would be all over the palace.

"How much?" I ask.

The man laughs. "How much what? I am asking, what do you have to offer that is equal in value?"

Absolutely nothing. All I have on me are some weapons and the clothes on my back. The Wazir, Ameer, was not happy about it—but I wasn't about to walk out into the unknown without the slightest bit of protection. Especially when I have Alara with me. I haven't forgotten my promise.

I step back, to walk away, but the man makes a sound with his tongue. "How about these earrings, for your wife?" He holds up a pair of pearl earrings that dangle on a small chain.

I nearly choke when he calls Alara my wife. She tucks her hair behind her ears, her cheeks red.

I turn back to the man. "I would, but I have nothing to give you. I can't give my weapons because I need to protect her."

He laughs. "Protect her from what?"

I look around, at the people who walking up and down the wide street lines with stalls. All of them are calm, laughing and present. None of them have weapons, or seem the slightest bit concerned for their safety.

But they are from here. I am not. They are every day people. I was raised and trained to fight.

When I don't respond, he places a cotton shirt down over some of the other trinkets that he has in his stall. It is probably a size or two smaller than me. "I will trade you these earrings and this shirt, and in return you will give me your shirt. It is silk, which is rare."

I look at Alara again. "Do you want them?"

Her expression shifts, as if I asked the most insane question. "You can't just take off—"

That's not a no.

I lift my hand to the back of my neck and slip the soft shirt off, over my head. Alara's gaze lowers to my body, her lips parting, before she quickly looks away.

From the way she is breathing, I know the image of me is still in her head.

I hand the merchant my shift and he gives me the too-small shirt and the earrings. The shirt fits closely, like second skin, squeezing tightly against my biceps.

I flex my arm to test that it won't tear with sudden movement, but the material moulds with my skin and doesn't rip.

"Can you stop?" Alara asks, her gaze on the compact sand that covers the streets here.

"Stop?" I step closer to her, intending to give her the earrings, but she quickly shifts away, her gaze lifting to the people on the street who pass us. A soundless laugh leaves my lips. "Why are you getting shy?"

I step closer again, but this time she doesn't move. My finger tilts her chin up, and her gaze goes from my eyes to my biceps, her lips parting again.

The way she is looking at me right now, like she wants to devour me. It makes me want to pull her so close.

Fighting every urge in my body, I stop myself from touching her further and instead I lift my hand to reveal the earrings to her.

Her fingers lift to my hand, tracing over the earrings. "Beautiful."

"They are yours."

She takes one and clips it onto her ear, followed by the other. They look perfect on her.

She deserves a compliment. "I—"

She wraps her arms around me. The force of her hug is so strong that it would have knocked me over if I wasn't trained to know how to keep my balance.

I hold her close to me, the feeling of her against me is strangely . . . comforting. Comfort is something I have not felt in a very, very long time.

"Thank you," she says against my chest.

It boosts my pride, that I could give her something that she likes. The feeling of deep warmth, like a plate full of samoosas on a cold night, fills my bones and my head.

My eyes are suddenly drawn to a golden dome that peaks out from behind the simple clay houses and bustling stalls that surround us. "What is that?" I ask.

Alara pulls away and follows my gaze. "I don't know." She starts walking towards it, and I stay close beside her, wanting to tug her arm and keep her behind me.

It's a round building, with a wide open arch as a door. People socialise outside and inside, people sit seeming to be reading or praying.

The golden dome is bright, seeming to be lit even without the sun around. To the left side is a tall minaret that points up into the sky.

My hand falls on Alara's lower back, guiding her towards the minaret steps. "Where are we going?" she asks, her eyes on the people we pass.

"Up." The best way to asses a city or area, is from above it. Instead of wondering the streets, we get the entire map of every street as far as our eyes can see.

At the top, the view is like a reflection of the stars. Buildings and lights flicker and blink. Something I never in my life thought I'd see—light, without fire.

But how?

Alara sits, her legs dangling off the side of the wall. I sit beside her, close enough that our shoulders touch.

The air here feels different, fresher. Behind the dome, on the edge of the city, is the ocean which drifts off into a shadow of darkness.

"Is it hard?" Alara asks, seeming to speak more to the night sky than to me.

I hide my smile. "That depends on what you're talking about."

"Losing a parent. My dad left, and I don't know if he is dead. But it makes it easier knowing there's a chance he could be alive." She looks over at me.

"I never knew my mom. I have the faintest memory of her face, mostly based on paintings I've seen of her, but she died when I was five." I can still see her face in that painting I found in one of the hidden rooms of the palace. It was dusty and scratched. Her face looked sad in the painting. She was holding both Nawaz and I. "It is hard to not know her, but it is harder to know my father. I don't know why he doesn't claim me as his own."

"Would you want to be the Hakeem?" she asks.

The only reason I would want it, is to know that Nawaz wouldn't be in control. He would most likely spend his days wasting money, and his nights with wasted women. He wouldn't be a good ruler, and the people of this land deserve a good ruler.

I just don't know if that would be me.

"If you could be royalty, would you want to be?" I ask, avoiding her question.

"Probably," she says. "I wouldn't have to worry about getting food. I would get to help my mother, to make her smile for once. Maybe I could buy her a beautiful dress." She sighs, her eyes becoming glossy. I wonder what she is imagining.

"That sounds nice."

She nods. "Dreams always do."

I shift closer to her, wanting to comfort her. For some reason, the idea of not kissing her makes my heart ache. I reach my fingers up and tuck her curls behind her ear.

My teeth graze against my bottom lip. She looks down at my lips and then back into my eyes. She looks so beautiful, the lights reflecting in her eyes.

Maybe it's the beauty of the moment, or maybe it's her.

My thumb brushes against her cheek. Her skin is soft. She leans into the touch, her eyes falling closed. I want to kiss her so badly.

My fingers slide down, slipping behind her neck. It couldn't be that bad, to kiss her. I tuck her face closer. Her eyes fly open.

Ah man. I'm only lying to myself. It would be bad. It would change everything. I move back. "I'm sorry." I turn away to look at the skyline. I wish I didn't think so much about consequences. "I don't want you."

But I know that if it was any other woman, I would still want there to be a closeness between us, solely because of the amount of time we are spending together.

It's not her. It's just the situation.

"I know," she says softly.

My head snaps to hers. Her fingers nervously fiddle with her clothes. That wasn't the response I was expecting. I thought she'd be hurt or angry or offended.

She meets my gaze and smiles a small smile. It barely lifts the corners of her mouth.

"You know?"

She shrugs. "You're royalty and a trained guard. I saw the way women here look at you, without even knowing your position. If they knew you were a part of the royal guard, they'd be all over you." That's most likely true. "And I'm . . ." Sadness fills her eyes. It makes it painful to not reach out and comfort her.

"You're what?"

She looks up at me with a 'duh' expression. "You've caught me stealing. You've caught me lying. You've seen my home. I'm nothing, Zayen. I shouldn't even be here."

My face flushes with anger. "You're not nothing."

The pendant earrings I bought her gleam in the soft light. They're beautiful. I hope she never takes them off. I hope she looks at them in the mirror, or traces her fingers against them, and thinks of me.

She says nothing, only nodding, but I can see she doesn't believe me. I don't like this feeling; to know that I value her as a companion and yet she thinks she's worthless.

"Don't say you shouldn't be here. It means to have faith. Faith that she is being lead on the correct path and she's exactly where she should be.

I won't kiss her, but maybe I could . . . I reach out and slide my hand over hers. Her chest jumps as she sucks in a breath, her eyes going to our hands.

I slip my fingers between hers and gently squeeze her hand.

She frowns, pulling her hand away. She says nothing, her head turning away. Why did she—? My voice comes out deeper and rougher than normal when I say, "Don't move away."

"You can't do this when you don't want me. It'll hurt us both. Please, don't touch me."

That's a fair request.

I hate it.

"Do you . . . Do you want me?" I want her to want me.

She stares down at her hands, and then up at me. Say yes. Her lips part, conflicted on the answer. "We should go."

She rises to her feet. But I saw it in her eyes. In the way that she studied my expression longer than she needed to. The answer.

She wants me.

CHAPTER 27

Alara: This place is incredible. I never knew it existed—although, I'm glad I didn't. If I needed money to help feed my mom and I, I definitely would have come here to steal and sell one of these lamps in Qadura.

It would have left me well off for a long time. I wouldn't have felt the need to fake being a royal and throw myself into the mess of a situation in the first place.

Zayen and I turn the corner and enter into another market. There seem to be different markets and stalls all over the area—way more than Qadura and Wadi combined. The smell is warm, like home-cooked food. It is filled with all kinds of foods, from bright fruits to crispy tamriyeh.

My mouth begins to water. Tamriyeh is a dessert I only remember having as a very small child. It is dough that is filled with pudding and then fried.

A soft cry for help draws my attention, and I push past a few people, not bothering to look back for Zayen.

A man holds a small child down on the floor, his face pushed against the sandy floor, while another man crushes the child's fingers with his foot.

He cries, begging them to stop. "I should take your hand! Your head!" The man's voice is like sandpaper. He looks vengeful, like he has spent years looking at everything with a deep frown on his face and now it is stuck like that.

"Ghalas!" Enough! I rush to the man, using the force from my running to push the man off the child's fingers.

The other man reaches for me and I duck out the way. He steps away from the child, and the child gets up and runs around a corner, disappearing.

People are staring already, but they don't seem to do anything. Why? The man grabs for me again and I duck away, straight into the other man. He holds my arms tightly behind me, the position uncomfortable and painful.

But not as painful as the realisation that I am in this situation again. My heart caves. Maybe this is never going to end.

Zayen is nowhere to be seen. I search for him, but I can't find his face. If he saw, I know he'd help me. He wouldn't run. He promised he would protect me.

Right?

Maybe he left because he could see how badly I wanted his arms around me on the top of that minaret. I didn't crave to be kissed or to be touched, but to be loved and caressed. By him.

For a moment, when he had asked if I want him, I had imagined him pulling me in close and letting me rest my head on his shoulder or his broad chest. I remember how comforting it was to be carried by him before, and it would have been a thousand times more so if I was cuddled by him.

But, as the man jerks my body back, it is a startling realisation that Zayen is gone. Whether by mistake or on purpose, I'm on my own. And stupidly, I still didn't learn how to fight—even after the many reasons I've been given to learn.

Even the tactic I used before, of trying to use my body as a weapon, doesn't work here. Maybe it's the distraction of knowing that I am completely on my own, and I don't have anyone who will have my back.

As if I am back in the streets of the souk again, having to fight for myself because nobody else will fight for me. I am that girl who steals because nobody else can provide for me. Nothing has changed, even if everything is different.

The feeling of loneliness crushes me as the second man comes to stand in front of me, his towering form nearly making me step back into the first man who holds me from behind.

His gaze leaves mine and calmly looks around at the people walking by who stare at the scene, but do nothing. He knows they won't try to do anything. He is nearly as big as Zayen. I wonder if Zayen would have—

"Yalla," the second man says, nodding his head to the side. And then I am being dragged across the floor. The foods and fruits in the stalls all become a blur of colours as tears cloud my vision.

I want to scream, I want to fight, I want to do absolutely anything but my body feels numb. I didn't want to lose hope, but I have nothing to hold on to.

So I stop letting my legs drag and choose to walk. I follow them. My heart sinks deep into my chest, making it much harder to take each step forward.

There's no way to tell what they'll do—how angry they are. The man's grip on me is tight, knowing that, like anyone, I would run if he loosened it.

I'm not a fighter, I'm a runner. So I'll have to wait for my chance to run.

"Where are we going?" I ask.

The second man—the tall, seemingly grumpy one, turns to watch me closely. The look in his eyes feels like it is boring into me. It reminds me of the way Zayen used to lock at me. "That depends on you." His accent is thick

"Please let me go. I don't have anything." My steps slow, trying to waste time to look for an escape.

He grunts. "Oh, so now you are trying to reason, but when you were stepping into our punishment you didn't bother to ask why we were doing it?"

"He is just a kid!" I nearly trip over my feet as the first man pushes me along. I want to kick him, solely because I am already walking and being compliant. There is no need to push me.

"Yes, and kids need discipline or they will turn into horrible adults."

"Breaking his fingers is not—"

"And here you are again, still arguing when you don't know the context of our actions." He whispers under his breath, calling me uneducated.

An insult that that lands it's hit. "Fine, why were you punishing that kid?"

"He was constantly getting into fights, bullying other kids and stealing from them without consequences. His father refused to correct him, so we took action. If that child doesn't learn to do better, he will not change."

"Okay, please let me go now." I dig my feet into the ground, trying to stop, but obviously that doesn't work.

"Every action has a reaction. You chose your actions, now you will follow us."

"Where are you taking me?"

He puts up his hand, walking ahead of me. And that ends our conversation.

Eventually we come to a boat sitting at a small dock, and my heart sinks. It's a wooden boat, only able to fit three or four people. "Wait." I push back, fighting my way out of the man's grip. His hold on me tightens to become painful. "Wait, no! I can't leave."

My mom. I can't leave her here. Using my elbows, I fight and push and make it as hard as possible for them to get me onto the boat.

The second man grunts and lifts my legs as I kick. "No! No! Stop!" I scream on the top of my lungs, if only to irritate them into not wanting to spend a boat ride with me.

They dump me onto the boat and untie the ropes to release it into the water. I turn back, to look out into the empty ocean where nothing can be seen except water.

The boats shifts slowly with the current, and I lean over the side to watch the dark blue that shifts beneath us. It's terrifying to not know what is down there, to not know when it ends.

But not as terrifying as having nobody, and no idea where I am going or what will happen.

My plan of running won't work now, so I'll just have to change my plan; survive. That's all I have to do—and it's the one thing I'm good at, living against the odds.

The sun peaks out from behind the clouds. It warms my skin. I stick one hand into the water and the current rushes around it, moulding against it.

The second man, the taller, more intimidating one shifts closer to me, watching my hand in the water. His brows furrow. "You'll be okay," he tells me.

"I want to go back. I want to go home." Although I have no idea where home is anymore.

"You're going to somewhere better."

"W—" My heart soars into my throat as I am thrown over the edge of the boat, my head plunging into the freezing water.

Chapter 28

Alara: Kicking up, out of the water is impossible. It is like a vacuum of water, sucking me down no matter how much I try to go up.

Water fills my nose, my lungs, every part of me. I try to hold on to my life, but with each second that passes it becomes harder.

The salt in the water burns my eyes. I twist, my hair tangling around me as I go deeper and deeper into the darkness.

Each time I move, the water seems to light up with small sparks of blue. The more I struggle, the more it envelopes me.

My lungs burn like they have been dipped in acid. Bubbles leave my lips—each one a signifier of the air that I no longer have. Until there are none left.

For a moment, I feel weightless, my head feeling so dizzy and lightheaded that the darkness I am submerged in seems to come alive with colours and light.

The colours dance and move, like gentle lights in different shades of blue. It is magical, like how I'd imagine it would be to fly out into space to watch the stars dance.

There is no way this is real. Is this what happens after death?

My body keeps being sucked down. I cough out the water in my lungs, and my body automatically inhales more in. It burns all over again, the pain making me cry on air I don't have.

My hands fly to my throat, tears filling my eyes only to be washed away by the stinging salt water.

I cough out more, the water tasting like acid. It hurts so much. From every direction, the pressure of the water seems to squeeze me. Please, please, please. I want this to be over.

The force of the water seems to lift for a moment, before I am plunged into it again—this time, it is not salty.

I'm barely able to kick up, but some sort of survival instinct gets my head above the water. I hold onto the strange silver outer lining of what seems to be a pool, hurling all of the water out of my body and onto pure black stone floors.

I can hear sounds but they're muffled by the deep ringing in my ears. A deep pain throbs at the back of my head. Somehow, I'm alive.

Each breath I take, even without salt water in my lungs, burns like I am breathing fire. A woman steps in front of me, holding out a glass of water. I am going to kill her. Why would I possibly want water right now?

Her tinted pink lips move, and I can hear the gentle muffle of her voice, but I can't hear anything.

She helps me over the edge of the giant tub of water and I sink onto the cool black stone, my body feeling completely drained and empty.

"Where am I?" I try to ask, but I can't even hear my own voice.

From the expression on her face, she heard me—but for some reason, she is staring at me as if I swore her mother.

She turns, her white robe swishing, and speed walks out of the room too fast for me to stop her.

I try to lift myself from the smooth floor, but my arms feel weak, as if I did pushups non-stop for three days. Shifting onto my back, I splay my arms out at my sides and take deep breaths.

Okay, I'm alive. Possibly.

Another deep breath.

I need to figure out where I am, and then figure out how to get back to Diyar.

A frustrated groan leaves my lips. I just want to kick something; to squeeze something; to throw something so hard that it smashes into tiny little irreparable pieces.

Every time I think I'm taking a step forward, some nonsense happens that puts me one thousand steps back. Now the idea of getting back to my mom seems like a distant dream.

All I hope is that she doesn't think I abandoned her. Surely she knows that I never would.

Strong hands grip onto my arms, and suddenly I am being dragged across the slippery stone floor. That same woman who ran out before is now dragging me with the strength of two horses.

There is nothing to grab onto, and with the way she is pulling me I can't do anything. This must be the hundredth time I'd wished someone taught me to fight.

Then again, Zayen was trained his entire life on how to fight and yet there were many situations that even he could not escape.

I shout, even though I can't hear myself fully. She ignores me, continuing to drag me. I have a feeling she is going to lock me up somewhere.

All of the floors and ceilings here are the same black stone. Almost like we are in a cave, only it is perfectly polished.

I stop fighting when I realise the light that brightens the passages that she pulls me through isn't fire or sunlight—it is that same, strange blue light that Zayen saw in the souk; the same blue light that seemed to dance while I was drowning.

"What is that?" I try to ask, but I don't hear the muffled sound of her response. She has resorted to ignoring me now.

We stop in a dimly lit, hot room. Steam rises from a basin in the center of the room. Wooden panels line the walls like benches.

I stand, against my bodies wishes, when the heat of the floor starts to burn. The woman starts tugging off the robe I was given back in Diyar. Stepping away, I shake my head. My ears unblock and the sound of hissing steam is all I can hear.

She knocks my hands away and pulls off the robe, so that I have nothing covering me. My arms cross over my private parts, and she rolls her eyes, muttering something under her breath that I don't catch.

Finally, she turns her focus towards a bucket lying in a tub of water. She fills it to the brim and—My eyes squeeze shut as I am drenched, yet again, in water. Seriously?

At least the clean water takes away the burn of salt in my eyes. I rub the water off my face, as the woman rubs some strange, gooey brown substance between her hands and starts rubbing it all over me.

I jump back, nearly slipping. It's soap. She's washing me. "What are you doing?"

She continues, but I push her hands away. She gestures to my body and speaks with a frustrated tone, but . . . But I don't understand a word. I didn't think that was possible.

She continues to wash me, and I stand frozen in the hottest possible room. She gestures with her hands for me to sit on the bench that lines the walls. I stare at her, doing as she says.

She seems normal. Her facial features are soft and delicate, with pale skin and plush red cheeks—most likely from the heat.

But she couldn't possibly be from Qadura, Wadi, Ardifa or Diyar if she can't speak the language.

Once she's done, she throws a bucket of warm water over my body and starts rubbing a strange light creamy-white substance on my skin. It's slightly watery and smells earthy. Clay.

She says something in her language, and then gestures that I must wait. Then she turns and leaves, locking the door to the room.

Now I'm alone and naked in a dark, hot room with no way to escape and no way to understand what she wants.

If I'm being completely honest, I wouldn't be surprised if I had died in the ocean and now I'm in . . . whatever this place is.

I don't think they'd clean me and coat me in clay if they're going to send me to hell, right?

Finding a towel laying underneath the benches, I cover myself. "Astaghfirullah. Astaghfirullah. Astaghfirullah." I begin to pray, asking God for forgiveness. I wish I had never had to steal.

I stand and try the doors to see if they will budge open. It's so hot. I need water.

I search around, but find nothing. There is writing on the walls. It's the same writing from inside the cave in the mountain that I used before, to pass to get from Wadi to Qadura.

The woman comes back in and I quickly hide the towel back and sit. She watches me warily, looking around the room for changes as if, what? I'd place a hidden bomb somewhere?

She has very high hopes of my skills. Unfortunately, I have none, except stealing. She takes a glove and slips it over one hand, then starts roughly scrubbing at my body like she is trying to remove five layers of skin. I clench my jaw, glad that she is working fast.

Once she's done, I'm hit in the face with another bucket of warm steamy water. I wipe my face with my hand, my body dropping.

Ah. My skin feels amazing. I can't stop rubbing my hands over my body. It feels smooth and glossy, as if I have been soaked in the most incredible oils every day since birth and now I have skin equal to those of royalty—those with the pleasure of time to care for themselves.

She hands me a fluffy robe which I wrap myself with and then holds out a white plain piece of cloth, which she uses to wrap around my eyes.

She tries to explain something to me, but I only understand one or two words—one being 'bad' and the other being 'meet'.

Am I going to meet someone bad?

CHAPTER 29

Alara: I stumble along, uncertain of which direction I am going. I try to reach out, to use any of my senses to give me clues.

But I can't see anything with the blindfold on. All I smell is the scent of roses from whatever was rubbed on me.

I can hear the gentle sound of water flowing, as well as footsteps. Not just mine and the lady's. Several. Some heavier, some more in a hurry. But none of them speak, like they are all busy with something very important and consuming.

I was considering fighting this woman who bathed and blindfolded me, but considering there are other people around it might get me into trouble.

I'm not sure about the rules of fighting, but I'm quite sure being able to see would be a good start.

The woman's hand stays on my wrist as she guides me. Her skin is incredibly soft. I wonder if she scrubs herself as aggressively and she scrubbed me.

"How much longer?" I ask.

This is horrible. There's no chance she'll understand me, and even if she did I'd have no idea how to understand her response.

A door clicks open and then she is guiding me to a stop and removing my blindfold. I get a glance outside, before she closes the door, and I can't believe what I see.

So much greenery—impossible. This makes no sense. The houses are different too. Tall, white and strangely shaped.

She explains something to me in her language, gesturing to the room. From what I can understand from her gestures, she is saying that this bed and room is mine and that I need to stay here.

But then again, she could be saying that I must not touch that bed or I'll be killed. I wouldn't know.

It is a simple room, compared to the palaces. But after having slept on a mat for my entire life, it is perfect.

The bed sits, curtained by thin white veils on all four sides. It looks delicate and welcoming. The rest of the room is empty aside from a sofa and a door leading to what must be a bathroom.

The woman says something to me, her voice tranquil and calming. A small smile lifts the corners of her mouth. Then, she turns to leave and I quickly grab her arm.

She begins to turn back to me but, before I can overthink it, I throw her to the ground. She falls quickly, especially compared to the guards and giant men I have had to fight before. She tries to get up and I panic—I don't want to hurt her.

Instead of causing harm to her, I pull the door open and run.

It is an overwhelming sight. It sucks the breath out of my lungs. There's . . . No sky. No clouds, no sun. Nothing. It's like a cave, and where the sky would be is a strange but incredibly beautiful silver layer that seems to move and reflect light, like a silk blanket.

The buildings are like nothing I have ever seen before. They are tall and white and strangely shaped. They are what I would imagine a child would create if given clay and told to build houses. Completely off balance and morphed.

I want to get in closer, to see the strange detailings of the walls or to see what might be inside, but I don't stop running.

The feeling of running—my heart racing in my chest and the tightening of my throat—reminds me of the days when I would steal.

I've lived every day wondering I would survive to the next. I always thought that at some point that feeling would end—that I would make it out of cycle and stop having to run for my life. That I would get enough to make my mom smile again, and to buy a nice bed and some good food for us.

But I am still running, and the stakes must be way higher now. I don't know what the rules of the land are like here. They could do much more than kill me.

That keeps me putting one foot in front of the other, as I brush past many people who wear the same white outfits as in Diyar.

Am I still in Diyar? But what about the boat and being pushed into the ocean? I know what I saw. I was sinking, and I saw that same blue light that is in the hallways here. The same blue light that was, in fact, bottled up in lanterns in Diyar.

What is going on?

I want to scream and cry but none of that would help. There has to be someone that has answers. Anyone who can speak the same language as me or gesture to me or in any way at all explain to me where I am.

And for the first time in my life I wish for my old life back. I wish for the simple struggle of surviving one day at a time. Of coming home and seeing my mom sleep on the couch.

I really, really miss my mama.

I wonder if she would know what to do in this situation. If she'd have any advice to me. But for as long as I remember, she has been closed off—even when showing love.

People that I run past stare at me. The land seems huge and endless, but full of life and nature. Everywhere there is lush plants and greenery and fountains of water.

Every road and pathway is paved with black stone, but to seperate the road from the walking passage are small streams of constantly flowing water. That must mean that the city is built on a slope.

If I keep running up, in the opposite direction to the flow of the water, I'll find something significant. Something that may give me answers as to where I am.

I cross one of the roads, my legs starting to burn with the pain of the run.

A loud sounds comes from my right and I turn just in time to see a strange contraption heading towards me.

It's not a horse or carriage or anything that could possibly exist. It is similar to a bicycle but thicker and with large wheels at the bottom that spin, creating a blue light inside them.

The contraption makes another loud sound and I jump out of the way, but it still knocks against me, causing me to fly forcefully against the ground.

A searing pain shoots through me, followed by the crashing sound of the contraption against the ground.

I guess running across a road is not a good idea.

CHAPTER 30

Alara: A fuming man pushes the contraption off his leg and stands. Signs of an injury show when he limps towards me. He stays speaking to me—not with anger, but like a father would chastise someone he loves.

He's not old enough to be a father. He looks similar to the men who took me on that boat and threw me into the ocean. A dark beard, heavily tanned skin and a naturally intimidating facial expression. His eyes are like the other woman's—an intense green colour that I have never seen before. Not on Qadura or Wadi or any land.

He wears a loose white shirt and white pants. The knee area of the pants are now slightly dirty, after grazing against the ground.

Unsurprisingly, I have no idea what he is saying. "I'm sorry," I apologise, though it will be pointless. I suppose my luck is not good enough to find someone who can understand me.

His expression changes, his eyebrows lifting which causing lines on his forehead. "Yalla." He gently takes my arm. Finally, a word that I can understand.

He starts dragging me towards his tipped over bike, speaking to me hurriedly in his language. After fixing the position of the bike, he climbs on and waits as if expecting—no. I'm not going with some strange man.

My mom may have not taught me a lot in terms of formal education, but she most certainly taught me to never follow or trust strange men. She would say she'd have a hernia if I did—although I don't know what a hernia is, it doesn't sound good.

I take a step back. He notices my hesitance and starts rambling. But this time, I recognise the words 'Qadura' and 'Diyar'.

I nod my head. "Diyar, how do I get to Diyar?" I just want to go home. My mom is my home.

He points forward, making big gestures with his hands and trying to explain something to me. His voice is rugged and has a slight lilt, an accent I've never heard.

He is bigger than me. He most definitely could hurt me, but he has information that might be helpful.

I'm going to take the risk.

He shifts forward to make space for me on the back of his contraption. My heart pounds in my chest at the risk, and at the chance of finally getting some answers.

I get an aching feeling in my chest, wishing Zayen was here. I'd never had a male figure in my life, but when he was around I felt safe—like for once, I didn't have to fight alone.

The contraption seems to come alive. As soon as he starts it, the wheels begin to turn causing that same blue light to emit. It makes gentle whooshing sounds as it moves, like rapidly spinning liquid.

I nearly fall of the bike, trying to see the wheels, and the man chuckles and makes a comment.

He has a warm laugh that makes me want to laugh along with him. There are smile lines on the corners of his mouth and creasing the edges of his eyes which put me a little bit at ease.

We pass many buildings that are all the same; tall and white and unusual. The buildings seem to have pieces of grass and greenery growing on it, like it is alive.

People walk along the sidewalk, everyone looking completely normal and ordinary except that they wear the same white uniforms. A few other contraptions with the same blue spinning wheels go past. At crossing points, when the contraptions stop, the blue colour disappears and the wheels become transparent.

I nearly fall off the bike completely when a strange creature crawls along the side of the walkway. Because we are moving, I don't get a proper look but it looked like a crab, except much bigger and rougher.

My eyes go to the silver material that has replaced the sky. The reflections make it look like it is moving and flowing.

What in the impossible world is going on here?

Up close, I can see small details of the man driving me that I wouldn't have noticed from farther—the brushes of grey in his dark hair, the leathery texture of his skin, the tiny smudges of dirt on his clothes.

Let's hope he is not intending to kill me.

The land seems to go on forever—the same buildings and black roads with small flowing rivers along its sides. There is no way to identify one area from another, as if someone copied and pasted the same thing over and over.

The man's contraption comes to a stop outside one of the large white buildings. He gestures for me to climb off and then swings one leg over with a grunt.

He hasn't touched me once, which has made me feel much more comfortable and unthreatened.

So I follow him towards the building. The entrance is an archway with a glass door. Water lilies are hung up, possibly to create privacy.

But the building itself is a strange texture. Little indents go along the surface. I run my fingers along them. It's hard and rough.

"Marhaba, marhaba," he says, welcoming me to . . . his home? I don't know where I am.

But it is nice that he is trying to speak in a way understand, even if it's only one word.

Inside, the building is not what I had expected. It's a super-market, cluttered with foods and random items.

But the strangest thing of all is the blue spinning machines on the roof. As they spin, that same blue light shines bright, making me feel like I am still in the ocean. It's incredible and impossible.

The man gestures to all of the products and then taps his chest, explaining without words that the store belongs to him.

It's only then, seeing the fresh sandwiches in the glass casing and the fruits displayed in one isle, that I start to feel the empty hole in my stomach.

He waves for me to follow him. As much as I desire to walk through the isles and take something, maybe just a bottle of water, I follow after him as he limps ahead of me, through a back door. I don't know how I can make it up to him, for throwing him off his bike.

The room that he leads me to is small and dark, the only light coming from the store behind us.

There is a bed in the corner that looks exactly like the one I was offered earlier—crisp white sheets and thin white veils on all four sides.

Is there only one bed store in this entire place? And one architect with absolutely no creativity? And how the heck is the sky silver?

There is a gigantic bookshelf covering one wall, filled to the brim with books to the point that he had to make a new pile of books on the floor.

"Diyar?" I say. He knows about Diyar. I need answers.

He nods, pointing to his book shelf and gesturing for me to come.

Taking a second glance over the room, I notice things I hadn't before. Through the white veils on the bed, there is thick black rope lying on top of the sheets. There's no windows.

I take a step back, accidentally bumping into the frame of the door. There is no handle on the inside of the door. Alarm bells go off in my head. I really should not be alone with a unknown man in his bedroom.

He notices my hesitance and jumps to grab me. I scream, clawing my hand out to scratch his face. He roars in pain, sounding like an angered animal. There are new, red marks spanning across his cheek, stopping just before his upper lip.

We fall back against a stand of candy. It topples with us, giving him the advantage of being on top of me. He crushes me underneath the weight of his body.

No. Please. Nobody knows where I am. I don't even know where I am. Nobody will ever find me. He pins my hands to the ground, next to bags of sweets. The fear that courses though my veins is nearly paralysing.

With no options of weapons, I grab one of the larger bags of candy and tear it open with my teeth. The contents fall out of the top.

He says something in his language. In one quick motion, I shove the bag over his head. He goes to lift it up and I use the distraction to shove him off me.

There's no time to grab the rope, to tie him up, so I grab a giant jar of what seems to be pickled mango and knock it against his head as hard as I can.

His eyes roll to the back of his head, his body going limp. "No more!" I've had enough of people trying to take control of me, to gain power over me, to hurt me.

But I know it's not going to stop.

Leaning down, I press my fingers against his neck, checking for a pulse. His heartbeat pushes slowly against my fingers.

Now I take the heavy black rope and tie both his hands and legs. His body is too big and heavy for me to lift him off the bags of candy, so I leave him on the floor and go to the bookshelf.

It's too dark to properly read any of the titles.

I grab one and take it out into the light. Of course, it not in the right language. I keep going, taking books out into the light, until I eventually find one that I understand.

'Rules of Aleamiq'.

Chapter 31

Alara: I think I might be sick. The air here feels heavy and unfamiliar, like a deep sigh that hangs in the atmosphere, unreleased. Stepping out into the streets, I clutch the book I stumbled upon tightly under my arm, finding solace in its tangible presence.

There are more people out here now. I don't know why. A loud voice calls out over the city, in the same unfamiliar language.

I had say inside that store, half staring at the unconscious man and half trying to figure out the book I have in my possession. It spoke of a society governed by equality—where everyone dresses alike, resides in identical houses, and receives equal salaries. The concept leaves me yearning for a broader understanding of the world. It makes me miss Zayen. Since he grew up in the palace, he might possess insight into my location based on the information within this book. Yet, unlike him, I lack a formal education.

In simpler terms, I feel utterly foolish and out of place, like an ill-fitting thread amidst an intricate tapestry.

As I wonder the streets, the vibrant energy that now floods along with the waves of people, who all seem to be going to the same place, I trip over the stream of water that cuts through the streets, separating the road from the sidewalk. My foot is immediately soaked and I leg out a frustrated groan. Why is this even here?

A little farther along the road, a peculiar creature resembling a fish glides gracefully through the stream. Its creamy hue, adorned with brown stripes, and its ethereal, string-like tail add to its otherworldly aura. Wow, I am so glad to have refrained from drinking the water, for nothing within the book's pages mentioned the existence of these creatures.

Even the strange crab-thing from before. I may have seen a tiny crab on the beach once, long ago. My dad had an obsession with the ocean, from what I can remember.

But it had never been anything like the one I'd seen earlier.

The presence of this strange things only serves to further alienate me from the familiarity of home, amplifying the longing for my mother.

It feels like I am a puppet on strings, but the strings are being pulled in different directions and it's starting to rip me apart from inside.

Nestled between two pristine, white buildings, I stumble upon a small, cascading fountain. Its centerpiece, an astonishing sculpture of an open book, is unexpected. Usually men like to carve themselves onto fountains; I've never seen a book being placed with such importance before.

The fountain's water dances and twirls, cascading in delicate ribbons that release the faintest mist. The sensation of these droplets upon my skin rejuvenates and invigorates, offering a momentary respite from the unpredictable journey I am constantly forced to follow. The rhythmic splashing of water allows me to breathe and think better.

Carefully, I position myself to remain hidden from prying eyes, and sit to read.

As I delve back into the pages, each turn reveals more fragments of a broken puzzle. For all its revelations, it only deepens my curiosity.

There is something that occurs here called the Night Trials—a sort of competition where the people here work to complete different tests and trials.

My heart quickens with a blend of anticipation and trepidation. Where would I even begin? The weight of uncertainty hangs heavily upon my shoulders, my fingers lingering on the worn pages, eager to unearth the answers hidden within.

Maybe my education wasn't so bad after all. I am grateful for the fundamental skills I have acquired—reading, swimming, and the ability to navigate the basics of life. It has gotten me this far.

With each turn of the page, I unravel about the existence of the Night Trials. Apparently, it is a renowned competition where the winner of the trials is granted a wish. Does that mean that I . . . Is this the stone that the Hakeem wants? A wish granter.

A rush of thoughts floods my mind as I contemplate where to begin. Maybe I do have a chance of getting out of here.

Before I can organize my thoughts, rough hands seize me, abruptly lifting me to my feet and confining me in their grip. A surge of fear and panic courses through my veins, yet the weariness that engulfs me numbs my will to resist. At this point, I will give in to whatever fate awaits me—be it confinement in a dark room or living solely on peanuts.

I don't like peanuts.

In front of me, a familiar figure emerges from around the corner. It's Akilah. Despite her being a liar and a traitor, a sense of relief washes over me upon seeing her. She has the answers to everything I want to know.

"Akilah," I exclaim, a mix of gratitude and surprise tinging my words. The tension in my chest dissipates, a burden lifted. "Thank goodness," I mutter to myself, acknowledging the unanticipated relief her presence brings.

A sly smile graces Akilah's face as she raises an eyebrow. "Never thought I'd hear that coming from you, ' she quips, her voice a surprisingly soothing balm to my ears.

Understanding her words feels like a comforting embrace. "Me neither," I reply, grinning.

I can't help the happiness that I feel, like honey filling my veins.

Her subtle nod prompts the men to release their hold on me, although they remain nearby, vigilant and ready to heed Akilah's command. There's no time to wonder what kind of position and power she must hold here, to have guards at her back and call. All I want to know is—"Where am I?" My voice is laced with equal parts curiosity and desperation.

A burst of laughter escapes Akilah's lips, causing her eyes to crinkle at the edges. She gathers her braided hair to one side and gazes towards the road. "That's a tough question to answer," she replies cryptically. "Let's return to your quarters. Take a shower, calm down, and then we can talk."

Calm down? The words evoke an urge to cry, an overwhelming weariness at the unpredictability of where I am. I yearn for familiarity, for a sense of consistency, yet my options remain limited. Seeking answers has proven treacherous in the past, leaving my heart tightening.

Maybe I don't want to know the answer. I had never considered that.

"Fine," I give in, my voice laden with resignation.

She nods slowly, an air of elegance emanating from her. I notice that she now wears the same white attire as everyone else. The same one I was shoved in after a being scrubbed by that strange lady. It seems that being a part of this world demands conformity.

"Tell the guards when you are ready. They won't understand you, so just give them a thumbs up, and they will lead you to me," Akilah instructs before leaving.

I nod, but my focus remains on the room. It's the same one I escaped from earlier—an unassuming space with a single curtained bed and simple drawers. Nothing like the palaces from before.

The bed is inviting, and the weariness that engulfs me reminds me that I can't recall the last time I had a proper rest.

Exhaustion weighs heavy on my eyelids, and the strain of holding back tears only adds to my fatigue.

Turning on the shower, the sounds of the water manage to remove the negative, restless feelings bubbling inside me.

The shower itself is quite beautiful—an open design, unlike anything I thought could exist. In Wadi, my mother and I would use buckets and a cloth for our baths. Even in the grand palaces, I hadn't seen this.

Stepping into the cascading water, I feel it permeate every inch of my being. My eyes close instinctively, and the warmth and privacy offered by the shower embrace me. A bar of soap rests on a small ledge built into the corner of the walls. I glide the soft bar over my body, relishing the way it lathers and cleanses me.

This. It feels like being enveloped in a hug—something I have not felt in a long time. It makes me miss Zayen; his strong arms and grounding smile. The warm, spicy scent he carried.

I hope he is okay.

Once I finish bathing, and changing, I pull open the door to my room. Both guards stationed outside turn their gaze toward me, their posture rigid and harsh.

I give them a thumbs up.

I'm ready—even with knots twisting in my stomach—to get some real answers. Finally.

CHAPTER 32

Alara: What I come face to face with is not what I had expected. The most incredible buildings I have ever seen.

I'm almost out of breath by the time we finally reach the peak of the incline we had been walking up.

The guards walk along the roads like it is completely normal, as do the other people who walk past—but wow.

The three buildings are made of the same white material as all the other houses. The three buildings seem to curve around a fountain and from that fountain there are different streams on the floor that all lead off in different directions.

It's the same streams that divide the road from the sidewalk; the same water that connects the whole city, it seems.

This is so cool.

I've never seen anything like it. It—It scares me, because if something like this existed in Qadura or any of the lands nearby, it would be something everyone knows about.

But then again . . . The lamps in Diyar, that blue light, wasn't known by anyone in Qadura or Wadi.

I glance up at the sky. The silver sky. How is that possible?

For a moment, I stop and stare. It's so far away that I can't figure it out. Even back at home, most of nature is a mystery, but this . . . it's impossible.

My mind feels scrambled and exhausted, trying to figure out what question to ask Akilah first.

I am lead towards one of the buildings. They are all different: one is smooth and without markings or indentures, one is made with lots of angles and edges and has a lot of glass windows looking out. The last of the three is the most beautiful one I have ever seen.

It's unexplainable. Whoever did this is unbelievably talented and dedicated. There are the most intricate details of the ocean and it's unknown creatures which I've never seen. It must have taken years to complete.

The guards take me towards the second one; the angled and jagged looking one.

The texture of the building's exterior is rough, like the bark of an ancient tree. Each angle and edge seems purposefully carved, as if the building itself is a work of art. I reach out and run my fingers along the rough surface, feeling the intricate details etched into the walls.

One of the guards turn to give me a stern look, because I am already touching things I am not supposed to, so I quickly pull my hand back to my side.

The people here all seem perfect and beautiful; the guards who have perfectly angled faces and clear skin. Their hair is all dark. They seem very clean, but it could be because they wear white.

As I enter through the massive doors, a surge of excitement mixes with my nervousness. The interior is a stark contrast to the outside. Soft, warm lighting illuminates the spacious foyer, casting a gentle glow on the polished white floors. Looking closer, I notice that the floor is made of stone and there are pieces of different coloured rocks and crystals mixed into the white.

The air carries a faint scent of something unfamiliar yet inviting. It's is like fresh ocean air and vanilla ice cream. Strange. It feels like a memory.

I take hesitant steps forward, my eyes darting around, trying to absorb every detail. The walls are adorned with screens that move and project different images and tell stories of their own.

This—What? How?

The nervousness in my chest gradually gives way to a sense of wonder as I continue deeper into the building.

The sound of distant voices and the soft hum of machinery fill the air, adding to the atmosphere of the unknown.

I'm supposed to be following the guards, but as they lead me down a hallway, there are different rooms with windows looking in. I stop, wanting to curb my curiosity.

Each rooms filled with peculiar contraptions and intricate mechanisms—which only leaves me with more questions for Akilah. I can't help but marvel at the ingenuity and craftsmanship that went into this. I want to explore all of it.

People are inside the rooms, hard at work and barely noticing anyone is watching them.

The sight of all these new things is both mesmerising and terrifying, in this strange world that I definitely do not belong in.

A part of me feels that by the time I am am standing in front of Akilah, she is going to laugh at me and tell me that I am, in fact, dead. That she's not really here and this is all just my mind playing tricks before everything blacks out.

But I don't want this to end, strangely. I want to know more about these buildings, about the endless contraptions in these rooms.

It has sparked a strong desire to unravel the secrets that lie within this city.

The guards finally stop in front of a grand door. Both sides are already open, but they shift to each side of the door and gesture for me to enter.

Taking a deep breath, I clench my fingers into fists, my heart racing like a horse on drugs.

The room I step into has walls that are filled with books. In the middle, it seems like a lecture hall or class room with rows and rows of desks.

At the far, far end is a window that looks out over the city. It is beautiful.

Akilah sits there, at the table with some strange black block in front of her.

"It must be beautiful at night," I say, staring out at the view. When it goes dark and that blue light might be spotted among the buildings.

Akilah looks out. "I imagine it would be beautiful, although the sun doesn't set here."

"What? Why—? What?" My brain is like a blank paper needing more; needing ink or words or paint.

"You haven't noticed that the sky is silver?" she asks, almost jokingly. "There is no sun."

"That's not possible."

"Is that not true for everything you have seen here?" I think back to the creatures, to the new language, to the blue light.

I say nothing. "How is there no sun?"

She tilts her chin up. "Because you're under the sea, in Aleamiq. Marhaba." Welcome.

And suddenly that feels true, because I can't breathe. It feels as if I am drowning. I can't bring myself to even fake a laugh.

"You're joking." No, I don't want this. This is not what I signed up for. None of it is. "How do I get out? I want to go back."

"You'll go back, and then what?"

I spin around, wanting to scream. I turn back. "This is insane!"

She nods and leans back in her seat, saying nothing. Her reaction makes me feel like I am insane for freaking out.

But she's right, I can't have gone through all of this for nothing. "That . . ." I point in a random direction. "That book. It spoke about a wish. The . . ." What was the name?

"Night trials."

"If I can get a wish, I could wish for something to get me out of this mess, right?" She stands, turning to look out at the view. I step closer to her, urgency and fear making it feel like I'm buzzing. "Right?"

She laughs and turns to look at me. "It's in two days, and you have no experience of this world. You couldn't possibly win."

"But I could try." Because what else is there? What else could I possibly do. It's the only option.

Her gaze turns to me, and it makes me want to melt into nothingness. Her presence has changed. She feels different, more confident and sure.

"Fine." She picks up her strange black block contraption and starts walking away.

"Wait," I call. She turns, raising her eyebrow. "Aren't . . . Can you help me?"

"You are the kind hearted one, not me, Alara. It is in your name. I choose to be smart, for it is in my name. You're on your own." She says something in the language of this land. Wait, can I call this land if this place is under water? "It means good luck."

And with that, she walks away. I stare at her as she disappears out of sight. The guards follow behind her.

Two days. That's it? How I am I even supposed to know when two days pass? The sun doesn't even set here!

A scream bubbles in my chest. I want to slide to the floor and just never get up.

But my mom. If I never go back for her, what will she think? I'm not giving up, for her.

Chapter 33

Alara: One day left.

I haven't slept. I've been in this building, surrounded by books and strange devices. My brain hurts, but things are slowly starting to make sense.

In the trials, they test three things: science, technology and art. I'm good at none of those.

I'm screwed.

If they would ask me to run, however, I would ace it. I've been running my whole life.

My brain is on overdrive from the amount I have been thinking. It all feels pointless. These trials are designed for people who grew up here, whose brains have been trained to think the way these trials want them to think.

If I don't get this wish . . .

A loud horn goes off, blowing so loud that it makes the floor vibrate. I stand, looking around, but there is nobody.

Going through the hallways that the guards had lead me through yesterday, I rush forward to the source of it, curiosity pushing me faster.

Why would they blow a horn? It has to be an emergency. At home, they'd ring bells to indicate a fire or weather issue.

What would a weather issue be here? An underwater tsunami? A sand storm?

When I reach the front door, I have to push my way out through the crowd. What the heck is this?

I don't bother to ask anyone, because they wouldn't understand me and it might just highlight me as an outsider.

Rig he now, I'd rather blend in.

They're all wearing beautiful clothes; whites and creams. It almost seems like a wedding except everyone is the bride and groom. They're so elegant.

I'm wearing a plain white pants and top that was left for me in my room. I threw my hair into a bun because I needed to spend my time preparing for the Night Trials that start tomorrow evening.

People are gathering around tables and eating different kinds of delicious-smelling foods. There are white tables lined with more food than I've seen in my life, even at the Hakeem's ma'duba which feels like it was lifetimes ago.

I have no idea how long it's truly been. It could have been days or months. I spent so long trying to get out of a routine and now everything is unexpected and I wish I knew what would happen next. For once, I just want things to not feel crazy.

The food. I can't stop staring. Plates and containers filled with all kinds of seafood and other things that I've never seen before.

Is it stealing if I take some, or is everyone allowed to have?

I forgot to eat today. I've always been used to skipping meals, so it means nothing, but to see this food . . .

My stomach twists. So I step forward and take a plate, dishing a bit of everything.

I try to move off to the side of the crowd and lean against the wall of the building I had been studying in.

People around are eating with their hands, so I copy them. As soon as the food is in my mouth, I'm melting. This is so good. No ways.

A moan leaves my lips and I immediately shovel more into my mouth, unable to wait for my next bite.

With a clean plate—I'd lick it if there weren't so many people around—I search for a place to put it. But nobody seems to have eaten as fast as I did. I walk over to the rows of food, wondering if I should take more food just to avoid standing around awkwardly.

A hand takes ahold of my arm. "Come."

His face is covered with cloth so that only his eyes show.

"What?" I ask. He speaks my language.

I immediately tug myself out of his grip, almost bumping into someone behind me. I am not going with a random person again. I have learnt my lesson.

I put the plate on the long table behind me, not caring if it's decent manners because I need both hands to fight.

It could even be him—the man who tried to lock me in his room. I knocked him out but didn't kill him. Maybe he is here to get back at me somehow. Or to take me back to that room.

"Yallah, Alara, let's go." He knows my name. I step closer, my heart tugging.

Why am I being vulnerable like this again, letting my guard down?

Because, there's this—He grabs my wrist and starts tugging me.

No! No, I can't. No more fighting. I try as hard as I can to resist, and eventually he turns to me, evidently frustrated.

He tugs me into his body. "It's Zayen. Obviously."

I stare at him, too stunned to point out that no, it is not obvious because his face is hidden.

"Zayen?" What? That's—How?

He nods and starts to drag me away. This time, I let him.

I stare at his back. His grip stays on my wrist. The white cotton shirt he wears fits his broad shoulders. Yeah, it's him.

When we make it away from the crowd, and the sounds of chatter and laughter is only a distant sound, he takes a turn down a narrower and shadowed passage.

There's another fountain. I guess the amount of fountains here makes sense, since we're under water. Does Zayen know?

"We're under water, Zayen. What do we do? This is insane? I keep getting this feeling that I am going to wake up and be in my house with my mom asleep on the couch and all of this being an insanely long and unending dream. But at the same time my imagination would not possibly make up something this insane."

Zayen nods, stopping to unwrap the turban from his head. He seems calm. Way too calm, so this isn't new information too him.

I shake my head, my heart racing. "How did you get here, because I got here through near drowning and then a random lady washed me and I was attacked and then Akilah—Akilah is here and there's this trials called—"

Zayen throws the cloth over his shoulder and steps closer to me, pressing me back against the wall, his chest pushing against mine. This brings back so many memories of us together.

I feel the rise and fall of his chest as he breathes deeply. "Alara, breathe."

Being here, with him pressed against me and his hands on mine, it takes me back to the day we met. He caught me stealing that necklace and pulled me to where nobody could see us.

He still smells intoxicating. I lean my head back against the rough, textured wall and stare up at him. He's the same, but different. His beard is shorter and his skin lighter—probably from the lack of sun. "How long have you been here? How much do you know?"

He shakes his head, his hand cupping my jaw. "We'll talk about all of that later, okay?"

"Later? No. We don't have time. The Night Trials. They're tomorrow. What are we going to do if we—?"

"Could you just shut up for a second?" He is clearly fed up. I'm not sure why, but I don't care because I feel like I am being caught in the middle of a tsunami.

"Shut up? Excuse me. Wh—?" His index finger presses against mine, his hands pulling my waist so that I am pressed up against him.

His arm slips behind me to hold me closer against him, but it is physically impossible to get any closer. My heart races with excitement, like a race horse headed straight towards him. It's been so long since we've seen each other. Finally, he's here.

He reaches out and gently brushes my hair behind my ear. I close my eyes, feeling his warm touch, and smelling his cologne. For some reason, having him this close makes me feel like I am closer to home.

Our breaths mix together, making me wish for more. His lips brush against mine, and all I want is to pull him closer and kiss him hard.

I won't give him the satisfaction of making the first move.

He smiles, as if he can read my mind and sense the stubbornness of my actions.

Then he kisses me, and my heart melts beneath a flame. Oh. I lift my arms, sliding them around his neck because if I don't my legs might give in.

It makes him chuckle against my lips. No, stop laughing. I want more. I kiss him harder, trying to show him without words how much I missed him and how glad I am that he is here.

He tastes like mint tea. It must mean that he has had time to relax; maybe he does have more information about where we are. I hope—I hope I don't taste like seafood.

The kiss gets deeper and more intense, making me forget myself. Everything falls away, his lips like a drug that I can't let go of. It feels perfect, the way his body presses against me and moulds against mine.

Zayn gives me one last, excruciatingly slow and taunting kiss and then pulls back. For a moment, there is nothing but deep breaths that fill the air between us.

The air feels charged with a thousand bolts of lightning.

He smiles, closing the space between us again. "I missed you," he breathes against my lips.

CHAPTER 34

Z ayen: Her panicked state reminds me a little of a chipmunk. If a chipmunk did hard drugs and didn't sleep for four weeks straight.

But I'm so glad to have her back in my arms.

"So . . . are you going to tell me anything? How long have you been here? Why are you here?"

I groan, running my hand down her face to try and quiet her. She won't stop talking and I just want to kiss her.

All I have done since she disappeared is talk and fight and try to figure out what the heck is going on—I literally went to the bottom of the ocean to find her—and now that she's here, none of the rest matters.

"We're going to steal." That's the plan.

"We, who? Steal what?" she asks.

"You and I, tomorrow, are going to steal that stupid wishing stone or whatever it is, and we're going to get out of here."

That's all I came here for; Alara and the stone.

I want to get Aya and Saad back. I want to make sure that they're safe and happy.

There's so many things I want. When I had lost sight of Alara, I had forgotten about all of it. All I could think about is finding her again.

But days have felt endless, and I've had more than enough time to think. I decided that I'll give the stone to my father. Whatever he wants, it's most likely to do with money and riches. He can wish for what he wants as long as I get those kids back.

"How?" she asks incredulously.

"It's kept somewhere hidden throughout the year, but during the competition, they bring it and keep it here"—I point to the Bayt buildings—"There are three buildings and they keep it in the technology building because it is the most secure there. It'll be in one of the rooms. So tomorrow before sunrise, we're going in and we'll take it."

"That's your plan? Go in and . . . take it?"

"Yeah . . ."

She sighs and steps forward. I reach out to touch her, slightly surprised that she is really here and standing in front of me after all this time. "Okay, I guess we've both got nothing to lose without our family."

But that's not true. I've got her to lose.

"So, we walk right in, take this stone and then what? We float up to the ocean surface, hand it over to the Hakeem and go our own ways?"

"Go our own ways? No, I—We can't see that far into the future, but I don't want to not have you in my life." I'm not sure about a lot of things—I mean, I think I saw a crab the size of two human heads a little while back—but her, I am sure about.

She nods and takes another step closer, her body inches from mine. I hold my arms open and she wraps her arms around me, her head pressing against my chest. "Okay, let's do this then. Do we even know how the inside of this technology building is laid out? I was in the for a little while but it is gigantic."

"Yeah, I met someone who is willing to help us."

She tilts her head to look up at me. Her big brown eyes seem to shine in the silver light here. "That is a useful piece of information that you didn't bother to mention."

I grin innocently. "I like to keep things interesting. Risky." I wink at her, leaning down to brush my nose against hers.

"Who is it?"

"I don't know."

"What?" She gives me a strange look and then laughs. "So this plan has absolutely no plan B or stability? What if we get caught?"

"Come on, have we had a plan B for any of this? It's not like we have a variety of options. We barely know anything about this place. It's another risk, but what else could we do?"

"Okay, but I want to go in alone."

"Not a chance."

She opens her mouth to argue, but then notices several people walking past. "Why don't we have this conversation in my room?"

"You have a room?" I slept on a strangers floor mat for the past three days.

She shows me to her room. I have no idea how she managed to find it, considering everything looks the same here.

It's a small space, but it has everything needed. I walk to the bed, about to fall over onto it, but Alara steps in my way.

I smirk. "What do you need?"

I don't know why being in here, in this small space, with her. It makes me want to—"You need a shower." She points to a door, the look on her face making me want to laugh.

I missed having her and her bossiness around. "Yes, madam." I bow formally, the way I once had to to my own father. A small smile tilts the corner of her lips up, but she doesn't budge. "I'll only go if you join me."

She wanted to discuss our plan for tomorrow, but if she has forgotten then I'm not going to remind her because there is no ways I am letting her go in alone.

"Not a chance." Her eyes widen.

I bite my lip. "I . . . sorry." I think not being around her has made me forget what our relationship used to be.

I head to the shower, immediately stripping down and getting soaked by the water. It's unbelievably good.

I step out, wrap myself in a towel and then realise I have a problem—"Alara!"

"What?" she calls back.

"I . . . Don't have clean clothes."

"Then put on the old ones."

"You're okay with me getting into your bed with—"

"No, just, uh—Just wait!" What, is she going to go out and buy some new clothes? "Are you decent?" she asks.

"I'm in a towel."

She pushes the door open slowly, peeks in like a baby duck going to a water hole filled with crocodiles, and then quickly tosses me a shirt and pants and shuts the door.

I laugh silently, shaking my head as I pull the pants on. They're stretchy so they fit well, but the top is not as easy. "The shirt doesn't fit!" I say through the door.

"What do we do?" she asks, opening the door only a crack, her gaze lowered to the ground.

"I could sleep without a shirt."

"And in the morning?"

"We have a lot bigger problems to deal with than my clothing choices in the morning. We'll figure it out."

"We'll figure it out' seems to be your plan for everything so far."

"Well, we're still alive aren't we?"

At that she looks up at me. There's a surprised anger in her face. It's kind of cute. "Barely."

That makes me laugh. Everything feels lighter when I'm around her, even risking our lives. I walk closer to her, and she immediately backs away from the door. "You scared of me, Sariq?"

She bites her lips, looking up at me through her lashes. Did coming to the bottom of the ocean make her prettier or something? "Sariq," she repeats, her voice barely a whisper. "I missed you."

"I missed you, too." When I reach her, I tuck her hair behind her ears on both sides.

She is wearing the earrings. The ones I bought for her. My fingers press against the pearl pendants.

Her expression changes and her hands go over mine. "The earrings." She laughs. "You traded your shirt for it." Her eyes go down to my shirtless body.

"Yeah, it was the . . ." The night we almost kissed. Wait, that moment just now . . . "Our first kiss. By the fountain. That was our first kiss."

Her eyes leave my chest to meet my eyes. Her cheeks turn slightly pink. "Right." She moves in closer.

My hands close around her hips, so that her body is flush against mine. Her hand goes to my bicep and quickly drops when she realises there is nothing separating our skin when she touches me there.

"Your, uh." She tries to tug away. "You have nice lips."

Her words contradict the way she is trying to get away from me. "You sure?" Everything else, sort of, doesn't feel like exists when she's this close. It's weird.

Her body stills, her eyes on my lips. "Yeah. I mean, I don't have anything to compare it to, but when you kissed me like you missed me, I liked that."

My hand cups her cheek, which feels as warm as I thought it would. Her skin is so soft. Her eyes flutter shut for a second, her body subconsciously leaning in closer.

I'm not going to kiss her now. Not in this small space, where we are alone and half-clothed. She has on a cute pink night gown—I'm surprised it's not white, too. Maybe white is only necessary when outside?

It would be too hard to stop once I start kissing her, so it's better to not start. Instead, I kiss her forehead and lead her towards her bed.

And that's where we stay, wrapped up in each other until her eyelids stop fluttering and her body and breathing relaxes.

Even though she's asleep, I kiss her forehead again.

CHAPTER 35

A lara: My feet knock against the ground as I run through the souk. There are men chasing after me. They caught me stealing a pair of fancy slippers from a stall and they're relentless. I must have been running for twenty minutes and they are still close, not giving up.

I can't outrun them. They're not stopping; not giving up like they usually do, even when I begin weaving through buildings.

I can still hear their footsteps behind me. "No, no, no," I say to myself. My mom. My mom. I need to get back to my—

"Yes, yes, yes. Alara. Wake up. It's time, and we don't have much of it."

I suck in a deep breath like I was stuck under water and I am finally set free. Oh wait, I actually am stuck under water.

Zayen's face is right in front of me, his hair falling forward as he looks down at me. He has changed and somehow found a shirt.

"How did you . . .?" My voice is groggy and I clear my throat, sitting up and rubbing the sleep out of my eyes.

How does he know? There's no sunrise here. There's no sense of time.

Everyone seemed to have chosen when they sleep in unison. It's such a strange place. How can they possibly live without the sun?

"No time for questions. We need to be out of here in five minutes. I'm worried the man who is helping us, who told me where the stone will be, might also rat us out so we have to be quick."

What? This plan is sounding worse and worse by the minute.

But, what else will we do?

For a second, my mind goes back to my dream. This is what I have always done: run. I've been stealing the things I want but don't have my entire life. It has always been to save my mom. That's what I was doing when I pretended to be royalty with the Hakeem, and it only put me in more danger.

Is this, the stone, really going to be what saves her?

When the Hakeem let's her go, and life goes back to 'normal', then what? Will we still struggle? Will I find myself back out in the souk, struggling and running and stealing again?

"Zayen, I—"

"Three minutes!" he insists, tugging on his shoes.

I throw of the covers, get ready and pull my hair back into a twisted bun. Running is always easier without hair in the way.

My heart feels like it is growing bigger and bigger, the feeling of it seeming to move from my chest to my throat and then the throbbing feeling shifts to my entire body.

Every inch of me is pulsing, shaking, but moving forward one step at a time to what Zayen called the Bayt buildings.

It's empty now, unlike when free food was offered. We waste no time getting into the building, where it seems to be free and available access for everyone.

Everything is dead quiet, and makes me feel even more uneasy. It's better to be able to see the threat, to know where to look and where to hide—but here, it's like this stone, which is obviously important, is being left with no security.

This doesn't feel right. "So we have no other plan?" The butterflies in my stomach seem to be getting out of control.

"This place is all out in the open. There's windows to see everything. If something comes up, we'll see it from a mile away. We're allowed to be in this building—anyone here has access. Just keep your head up. Keep looking for something that seems off."

"Something that seems off," I mumble to myself. That seems legitimate. Everything seems off. The sky is freaking silver!

I've been way too trusting, too reliable on feeling and it's lead me nowhere. Surely at some point I'll have to learn that just going with it doesn't really work.

But it's a lot harder to plan with zero access to information, so what else is there?

"There," I say, pointing to a closed door that has no windows looking in. It's the only one that seems to be more closed of.

My heart seems to finds its way into my throat, a rather common hiding ground it seems.

This feeling, I'm so used to it. It's what I always felt when I was about to take something I shouldn't; it's what I felt that day when Zayen caught me in the souk.

Being caught this time would have a very different ending.

Zayen goes in first, pushing the door open and it whines, giving us away to anyone that might be inside.

It's a room—a huge one. It's mind blowing. The soft grey walls are barely visible beneath gold framed mirrors and beautifully embroidered tapestry. The entire ceiling is painted, depicting scenes of war and love and music and food. There are several arches carved just below the ceiling, and on top of the arches sit small angels carved out of a hard substance. Inside the arches are more paintings, telling different stories.

Fires are lit on golden sticks that flicker inside the gold-coated room. This is incredible.

"Zayen," I whisper. It's impossible for this level of skill to exist. The tapestries are detailed all the way to the reflections in their pupils and the engravings on their armour.

"Blows your mind, doesn't it?" A deeper voice says. It's not Zayen's, but it's familiar.

In a golden-cream coloured sofa, sits the Wazir that we met in Diyar. The one who gave us fresh clothes and controlled Nawaz.

My first instinct is to run, and my body leans back ready to do so.

"How are you here? Is Nawaz here? How do we get back home? Did you do this—Did you send us here?" Everything happened so fast and there's too many questions and Akilah answered none of them.

He takes a deep breath. "Let us all be quite honest here. You were not in this building to get home. You were searching for something else. It's why you left the house in the first place, no?"

Akilah must have told him everything; that we are here for the stone to take it to the Hakeem. But I can't assume that he knows absolutely everything, so I say, "What do you mean?"

He laughs, and it's wheezy. "What are you looking for?"

The way he looks at me makes me feel like he can read everything that it is in my head.

His grey hair has been groomed. His beard about a fist length. "Who are you?"

"Who do you think I am?"

I half laugh-half choke. "No, but really? How are you here? You're the Wazir. What is this world?" Please, I want to add. Every day feels like I am sinking into sand and trying to grab onto something that isn't there.

"This is not a new world, it is simply a place that exists under water. It has existed for many centuries, created to be a land that is idea—no inequality, no violence, and a simple life. We still allow for creativity and innovation. That's why rooms like this exist." He gestures to the room that we stand in. "But it is not for the intention to boast, rather for the intention to show human capabilities. It's really not that complicated."

"Not complicated? There's no sun. How—?"

"Oh, you mean the fish?"

"The . . ." The fish. That's what the silver is.

"Yes, fish, that have created a dome above us. It's incredible how nature works. When they move, it creates rain which allows for water for our crops. Somehow things work, even when they shouldn't."

"And the blue light?"

"It's a type of algae we discovered that can create light. The scientist here in this building have been working to advance it—as well as some of the people competing in the Night Trials, which is where you should be if you need a wish."

So he does know. "I . . ." How do I say this? "I'm not good enough to participate."

"You are. You have gotten this far. Are you really going to stop now?"

No. Stopping isn't an option. Going back empty handed after all of this . . . Not an option.

"But it started today. We're too late."

"We will make a plan. Tomorrow, you and your . . ." He looks to Zayen.

Zayen looks drained. Their are dark circles under his eyes. His hair is still ruffled from sleep. I feel it too. Most likely because of the lack of sun that we are used to.

"Friend," the Wazir concludes. "Will participate."

I guess there is no plan B now, but there never has been.

CHAPTER 36

Alara: My shoes are barely visible, sunken deep beneath wet sand. We went east of Aleamiq and the heat is so intense here that I no longer miss the sun.

It feels like I have been going through empty deserts for seven years with no food or water—which I know is not technically possible, but that is how it feels.

The heat burns my skin, but I keep working, putting together a mix of all the ingredients that I need.

For todays competition, we're working on developing science.

Even though my body feels drained, my mind feels alive like it has been connected to the blue algae that creates lights here. Everything is buzzing and alight. We have access to everything here—all we have to do is open some kind of black technology device, find the product and place and order and they'll bring it right here.

So I decided to make a pill, combining different superfoods and vitamins that they have available to order. The things we put into our body have the biggest effect on us. So I'm making a happy pill.

I'd been up the whole night, stressed and not knowing what I will do. I didn't want to ask Zayen for help with brainstorming, because I could see he was lost in his own head about what he would do.

The people here have all the advantage of having time to prepare and being familiar with the land and what does it does not exist her. What is needed and what is not.

I had to think about what I needed, and what the people I have met above land needed; what my mom might have needed, to not end up sad and unmoving on a couch in a house with a bucket for a shower and a mat for a bed.

Happiness. A lot of it relating to not having enough, including in terms of health and nutrition. We ate what we could, not what we needed.

The technology they have developed here is amazing. They even have a pressing machine to combine all the ingredients together. It can make six pills at a time.

A positive aspect is that for these trails, they're looking for ideas to develop and not necessarily a whole and final product. Thank goodness, because if this isn't tested then I fear my non-educated, non-sciencey self might kill someone.

Something about the activity of combining ingredients at the correct measurements, mixing it all together and pressing it into a pill, makes the world fall away. There is no my world and their world, there is no above or below the ocean. There is just the task right in front of me, and something about focusing on something that I have control over helps me to let go and enjoy.

The air hums with anticipation as the deadline looms. There is a timer counting down the time we have left. One minute and then this competition is over.

Clinking tools, whispered conversations, and the occasional whir of machinery only make it feel even more tense.

A team of men delicately manoeuvre through rows of vivacious plants, meticulously studying their reactions to an array of stimuli. Each leaf and petal seemed to dance with life, responding to the scientists' gentle touch. It was a mesmerising ballet of nature and curiosity.

Across the space, a few others huddle around a web of interconnected screens, their faces illuminated by cascading lines of code. With every button pressed, they seem to light up with excitement, building sculpted, immersive realms where imagination moulds seamlessly with technology.

I shouldn't be focusing on them—especially with only seconds left, but the more I look the more I can't look away; the more I know that I don't stand a chance.

With each dwindling second, my heart races and my breath quickens. The climax of all this time feels like an unbearable weight.

This is all I've got. It's all I came for.

Then, at the stroke of zero, the room erupts into chaos. All participants are made to stand back, and not touch their creations. Judges dart from project to project, examining and evaluating the fruits of our labor.

The judges come to me and I gesture to the now compressed combination of powdered vitamins, and other beneficial substances.

My breath is shaky as I explain my ideas to them, but not nearly as shaky as my hands.

Throughout the room, a vibrant tapestry of creativity unfolds. The stage becomes a theatre of awe-inspiring innovations, showcasing the boundless human spirit. It reminds me of the room we found the Wazir in—the details and work in there was mind blowing. It is amazing to see what people are capable when given the space and the tools.

I bare my soul, tying to show them that the reason we need this pill is because we want people to want to live.

I've seen that this world prioritises people and equality and goodness. Surely a pill like this would be right up their ally. Hopefully.

As the whirlwind of presentations subsides, an air of anticipation settles over the room once again.

My eyes search for Zayen. I had forgotten he existed—forgot everyone and everyone existed—for a little while.

Now I am back in reality, and trying to figure out what the expressions on the different judges faces mean.

"Next round starts tomorrow!" One of the judges announces, and then like a pack of ants, everyone heads back to central Aleamiq.

Back in my room, the blast of air coming out of silver-lined squares in the wall feels like the most heavenly thing in the world.

I nearly drown myself, drinking a bottle of water and Zayen pulls off his shirt and falls forward face-first on the bed.

I stare at his back muscles, the tanned skin and the way sweat makes it shine in the flickering candle light.

Laa. Laa. Laa.

I don't need this. I need to think. I need to plan. Tomorrow is the design section of the competition and I need—

Zayen turns around. He leans up, his ab muscles flexing. He reaches out for me, his eyes pleading even when he says nothing.

I shake my head. "Zayen, no."

"Cuddles?" He reaches his arm out for my and my eyes stay to his biceps.

Being wrapped up in him sounds amazing right now. And I'm exhausted, but—"I need to think."

"Maybe you need to stop thinking."

"Zayen," my voice breaks. I sit on the edge of the bed. He shifts to be closer to me, wrapping one arm around me and pulling me into his side. The scent of him still lingers, even after such an intense day. It is familiar and comforting. "I'm scared. This is everything we have been working towards. Those people were competing with . . . they're amazing, and talented, and experienced. If we lose, if we have to go back empty handed . . ."

Zayen's face falls. In his eyes, all that welled up sadness seems to show. "I know. It sucks. I don't know what my father will do with those kids."

I lean further into him. It is nice having him here. Everything would be so much worse if he wasn't by my side, feeling the same things that I am. "You really love those kids."

"I do," he whispers. His lips brush against my ear. "And I love you. I'd fight anyone, and go to the bottom of the ocean to protect you, too."

And in a way, he did. He came here to find me.

With his hand, he tilts my face to be aligned with his. He places a gentle kiss against my lips and it leaves butterflies in my stomach and an ache in my heart.

He pulls back from the kiss and I nearly lean in for more, but he says, "Let's do this." He shifts back until his back is against the board behind the bed. He motions for me to sit beside him and this time, I give in. "Let's imagine we have the stone, what wish would we make?"

I'd been thinking about that for a while, because there's so many ways to ask for the same thing.

Would I wish for things to go back to the way they were? No. Would I wish for the Hakeem to be completely removed from the history of time? Possibly. "For our families to be safe and happy."

He nods, tugging me into his side. "For our family, and our land, to be safe and happy."

He is a true ruler.

CHAPTER 37

Alara: The bristles of my brush splay across the white sheet. What was a brown blob a little while ago is now forming and becoming what I had imagined in my head.

It makes my heart fizzle with excitement—to know what I am capable of outside of running and stealing and surviving.

Looking back at me is my mothers face. Even though it's been far too long since I have seen her beautiful, aging face, I still remember it as clear as the moment I hugged her goodbye.

There was such pain in her expression, in her eyes, and I tried to capture that in the lines that I trace across the sheet.

In my painting, the top of her head is cut open and images leak out of her like visions of the life she lived; the life we lived, and will likely have to go back to. That is, if we make it back successfully.

My eyes water as I take a very fine brush and paint in the details of our life; the cracks left on our walls, the bucket sitting beside piles of unwashed dishes. I also try to paint what I imagine would go through my mothers mind in the moments where she wasn't trying to sleep away her sadness.

I wish I knew more about her past; about what lead her to the life we had. A tear slips down my cheek. I don't want to go back to that.

ZIIIINGGG!!

A loud buzzer goes off multiple times, and then one of the judges—identifiable today by the badges they wear on their white uniforms—announces and gestures that we must step away.

Everyone drops what they are doing and steps back. I quickly fill in the blank space so that it does not look unfinished.

As I put my brush down, another judge comes to me, shaking his head, and placed a red dot on the top right corner of my painting.

I frown at him. "What does this mean?"

He tries to explain but I don't understand it. Only his gestures, when he makes a cross sign with his arms, makes me realise that I've been . . . I've been disqualified.

"What? No. I was just—it was just a tiny white spot. I can't—you can't—" Can he? "Please." I press my palms together, begging with my eyes.

He gives me a sad smile, pats my arm and walks away. I stare at the red dot. It seems to become bigger and bigger, until all I can see is red. Everywhere.

My breathing shakes. I try to turn, try to look around but all I can see is failure. I've failed. I've killed any chance I had of winning.

When reality finally comes back, I see a few other contestants looking at me sadly. This—It's not fair. I didn't know about the disqualification rule.

The paint hasn't even dried yet, and I have already lost everything. A cage closes around my heart, tightening and squeezing until it's too painful to exist.

My feet run before my brain can process any further. My shoes clap against the strange floor texture in this area, a stone-like substance.

I run until I am forced to slow down because the tears in my eyes are stopping me from seeing.

Tanaffasi! I need to breath.

As I am wiping my cheeks, strong hands grab me. My thoughts immediately go to that man on his motorbike, who tried to trap me in his store.

I pull back, but he keeps his hands locked on me. I look up. Zayen's talking to me but I don't want to hear him.

Seeing his face, the heartbreak that creases his expression, makes me want to run further. To run until I escape this land and find nothing but water and—"Alara." He is taking deep breaths. Something I wish I was capable of right now.

I glance up, wishing to stop crying. With each struggled breath, my chest heaves. The silver fish seem to sparkle as they shift, and drops of water land on my face.

I start laughing. The feeling eases the tightness in my chest for a millisecond. Rain? As the fish move and change their positions, more droplets fall from the sky, wetting our hair and out clothes.

"Why are you laughing?" he asks gently. Because it's the only thing stopping me from falling apart.

My laughter stops, my heart sinking so deep into my chest that I feel as if I can't stand anymore. My knees weaken and I hold onto Zayen, breathing hard.

What is happening to me? Tears fall freely down my face, and he quickly tucks me in his arms and hold me tight. "It's okay. I'm here. I've got you." His hands brush through my slightly damp hair.

Water continues to fall around us, but we stay still and silent. Until I say, "I failed. All of this. It's—it's nothing."

"It's not nothing."

I look up at him. "You? Did you . . . ?" Maybe he won.

He shakes his head. "I was trained as a guard. I'm the farthest thing from an artist. It's a mess. I'm . . . I'm sorry."

His shoulders slump, and he holds me tighter, sighing. He knows, as much as I do, that we have no chance now to save the people we love.

I reach out and brush a droplet of water from his cheek. He leans into my touch. The vulnerability that he shows; not hiding that my touch comforts him—it makes my heart lighten again.

Maybe we didn't lose everything. My hand slips behind his neck and I lean up, my gaze on his lips.

He brushes his nose against mine, his hands not letting go of me. "Are you sure?"

The rain is starting to make his shirt slightly translucent. My hands slide along the side of his bicep, then to his chest, then up to his shoulders. He watches me closely as I explore him.

"Alara," his voice is rough, much deeper. I quickly meet his eyes. Oh. The only way to describe his expression is raw and animalistic. "Stop touching me."

I bite down on my bottom lip. Challenge accepted. "No—" I almost fall backwards when he kisses me, but his arms wrap around me and keep me upright.

A small, surprised sound leaves my lips and it makes him groan. His one hand tangles in my hair and my fists tighten on the front of his damp shirt.

My heart seems to be beating only for him. Zay-en. Zay-en. Zay-en. "Hmm," I hum against his lips, wanting more. My whole body is losing feeling because it's all going to my heart.

He quickly pulls away, breathless, as if realising something. "This . . . This is a distraction. We need to . . . focus."

I don't want to. I don't want to focus on reality.

He sees my reluctance and adds, "We can't keep running, Alara."

"What do we do? Go back and tell your father that we failed? He's going to kill our family."

His jaw clenches. "I know," his voice is more of a growl than a human sound.

"We—"

"We don't even know how long we've been here." Frustration is evident in his voice. "He gave us a time limit. One month. It could have been longer. They could be . . ." He noticed my expression and shuts himself up. "Sorry."

The only image in my head now is the image of my mother lying with her throat cut, staring at the detailed carving of the Qadura palace ceilings; the chandeliers and the gossamer curtains, wondering why her daughter never came.

It becomes hard to breath again. I release my grip on Zayen only to realise I'm shaking. "Please." I don't know what I'm asking for. I don't know what I need.

His expression softens. He brushes his fingers against the back of her cheeks. He's shaking, too. He is just as scared as I am. "We can't escape this, Sariq. We have to face it. The least we can do is face it with our heads held high."

"Held high? Do you understand that those kids could be—?"

"Yes, I understand." His expression is tight. "Do you not think I understand? Every day, I woke up feeling like I didn't have a place in that palace, that I belonged nowhere. But with those kids . . . I felt like I had something to live for, and something to die for, and I couldn't even . . . I couldn't even save them." His eyes squeeze shut, lines forming between his eyebrows.

The pain on his face only makes this moment hurt more. I touch his cheek, wishing to ease the pain between us.

"We have to go back. There's nothing we can do," I say. We both know it, but saying it out loud feels too real.

"Maybe I can be of help."

Zayen and I put a good amount of distance between us. The Wazir walks towards us. He is in a white robe and has a badge, because he must be one of the judges too.

His sandals clap against the stone-like floor as he walks closer.

"I know that you two have good intentions coming here. That is what we try to influence in Aleamiq—kindness, generosity, virtue, humility, fighting for what is right. I see that in you, in your actions." He smiles, causing creasing at the corners of his eyes.

"So you'll, what, let us make a wish with the stone?" Zayen asks.

He laughs, the sound raspy and wheezy. "The stone is not real. Magic is haraam." Forbidden.

"So you lied?" I ask. "Doesn't that go against the values of Aleamiq. Honesty?"

"Morals are a tricky thing, are they not? The stone was only a façade for my safety, because the winner of the trails does get his wishes granted. Only it's not by magic or any of that nonsense—it's through me."

"Through . . . You?" This is ridiculous. No more ridiculous than breathing under the ocean, I suppose.

He nods curtly. "In this land there is no hierarchy; we're equals in land, in way of living, in what we have access to. But above water, things are different. I have boats, money, etcetera. If I can't grant their needs here, I can grant it above water. So, how can I help you?"

"Why would you help us?" He could grant this to anyone.

"Because, Alara, I'm..." One of his eyebrows lowers, and lines crease his face with concern. "I am your father."

Chapter 38

Alara: Wind makes my hair fly in all directions, as we sail towards the palace in Qadura. Having the faint glow of the sun on my skin again feels like a drug.

I take a deep breath. The smell of the salt and the air brings back some familiarity.

This moment is mine, it feels peaceful and beautiful and for once, I'm not trying to steal, I'm not trying to run, I can be still and simply exist.

Thanks to my father. My real, actual father. Now that I know the truth, I can see signs of it in the angle of his eyes and the curve of his smile. Or maybe it's simply because I'm looking for signs; for this to be true.

My fingers brush against the scar on my neck. I'd always thought it was a burn mark. It turns out, there are people who live between Aleamiq and Diyar; traders who move between the under water world and land. They're the ones who bear this mark, as it gives them access to both worlds.

There's so much about this land, about this world, that I have no knowledge of. I want to learn about all of it, and hopefully I can now that I know who my father is.

An arm slides around my shoulders, and someone pulls me into their side. I know it's Zayen without looking. I learn closer to him.

"We have a boat," he says. "Do we have a plan?"

I shake my head. "How is there any way to plan when we don't know what's waiting for us?"

Another set of arms wrap around both Zayen and I. "Lucky for you two, I do," Nawaz says.

He has a grin on his face that is so wide it might reach Qadura before us.

His royal highness has been living his best life, having access to the palace in Diyar and all it's luxuries, as well as being able to go out and explore the city as he pleases.

He has nothing to lose, so why should we trust his plan? It's unlikely that he'll go against his father.

"Let's hear it, then?" Zayen says. He watches Nawaz with reservation and hesitance.

"We have to kill my father."

Zayen and I glance at each other.

"While you two were loafing around, making art and love or whatever, I've been reading from the books in the palace in Wadi. My father has been lying to me about everything—aside from you being my brother. His plans, they . . . He needs to be stopped." He slaps Zayen playfully on the arm. "I say we take over, brother? What do you say?"

"Okay, but how do we stop your dad?" I ask.

"With your greatest weapon." Nawaz gestures to himself. "Surprise."

The endless trip back to the Qadura was painful. My father—if he's being truthful about his relation, although he'd have no reason to help me otherwise—lent us a ship and a map and a man who knows his way around the ocean.

But if the three day journey has taught me anything it's that the ocean is more dangerous above than it is below, with wild storms creating waves that nearly turned the boat upside down.

When my feet finally touch land again, I nearly fall over.

Zayen catches me by the elbow and steadies me, a small smile on his face.

"Don't look at me like that," I demand.

That only makes his smile grow wide. "Like what, habibti?" He still doesn't let me go, his touch calming in the wake of everything to come.

Even though we were stuck alone on a ship, I distanced myself from Zayen—busing myself with washing the decks and polishing spare weapons and absolutely anything to avoid looking him in the eyes.

Nothing has felt real from the moment Zayen caught me stealing in the souk, but reality is slowly creeping closer and I'm going to have to face it.

Zayen and Nawaz have been doing most of the planning, deciding how they are going to rule together and who they want in their court—Nawaz taking the lead since he knows the ins and outs of politics, with Zayen taking charge of handing the people and relations and making the land safer for its people.

They're both inspiring, and watching them has made my heart swell, but I know that I have no place in this world. When this is over, I'm not a part of their future.

I go back to my reality, hopefully with my mother at my side, and I will have to find a way to survive once again. Without Zayen.

The thought of it leaves a hole inside me. Distancing from him has felt more impossible than anything I have had to survive this far.

I want to reach out for him, to have him hold me again. There's something so lovely about feeling wanted. It's something that was too unrealistic to dream about.

The only sound that follows us in the streets, like shadows, is the slow crunching of rocks beneath our boots. Until that sound turns into something louder, fiercer—chanting, coming from . . . the palace?

When we reach the growing crowd, I see that it's not chants. It's a celebration. People are dancing and cheering and smiling.

We push our way through the crowd, but when people notice Nawaz, they part for him.

I watch everyone closely, but nobody is giving any clues to what might be going on. As soon as we are spotted, eyes shift to us, and they watch us like prey.

EPILOGUE

Zayen : Alara steps closer to me. She shifts nervously, looking like she fears that someone in the crowd might jump out and attack her.

As if I'd ever stand by and let that happen.

They are looking at us strangely. I have never seen them gather here like this in all my years. Maybe once, at the birth of Nawaz, but I'm quite sure the Hakeem did not just have another child.

Or maybe he did.

Inside, there are men that I used to see dining with the Hakeem. They all look towards Nawaz with sadness. There's a dullness to the place, that is certainly not coming from the gold-lined furniture.

Once we're lead inside the room where the Hakeem meets, I expect to see him there.

Instead, there is a letter lying on his low desk.

I take it, straightening to read it.

Welcome home,

This must all feel confusing. My daughter asked for my help, and I always do my job to the fullest.

Your Hakeem is gone.

The kids and Aaliya are safe. Aaliya returned to her home.

Maybe the kingdom will be better now, with a new ruler. It was wrong of me to think of Aleamiq as perfect and this land as criminal. It is not so simple.

Let's work together to make both kingdoms better.

Inshallah.

"He's dead. The Hakeem's dead." I push the paper towards Nawaz, then turn to Alara. "Is your moms name Aaliya?" She nods. "She's safe and at home."

Looking back at Nawaz, he looks shell shocked. His fingers tighten on the paper, causing it to crumple slightly. "This isn't how it was supposed to happen. I had questions. I had to know why." Frustration rolls off him in waves. It'll take time for him to process it. For everyone to process it.

Footsteps approach, the high ceilings make them echo, and Ali comes into view. "Yallah! I thought you'd slipped and drowned in a puddle! Here you are."

I immediately embrace Ali an he highs me back with the same amount of force.

Pulling back, my face in serious. "The Hakeem is really . . . ?"

"A pile of bones? Well, not quite yet but give his body some time."

"We need to get everything in order. Let me speak to my brother. We discussed a plan, but I guess it went differently."

"Your brother?" He looks at me strangely.

"Oh, yes. Nawaz and I. But where are the kids? Are they still here?"

"They're upstairs. First—" I don't even let him finish, already running towards the polished stairs.

The door slides open and Saad and Aya sit playing with little little clay toys on the bed.

They healthier and they seem older, even though Aya still has her squishy cheeks.

My shoulders relax as soon as I see them, my knees giving in and hitting the ground. They're alive. They're safe. I didn't want to let myself get my hopes up until I saw it for myself.

"Ba!" Aya calls and nearly face plants climbing off the bed.

They both run into my arms and a tear falls down my cheek when I wrap them in my arms. They're okay. They're okay. Knowing my father, I had been expecting the worst.

Aya gasps, pointing at the tear slipping down my cheek. It makes me laugh. Seeing her here makes me realise how much I missed her tiny, chubby face and those big brown eyes. She presses her finger against my tear and then looks at her wet finger in confusion.

I would give a gold coin to see what is going through her mind right now.

she whispers. Water.

"Where were you?" Saad asks. "You took forever."

I kiss his cheek and he cringes and wipes it away. Nine going onto nineteen, huh? He is so much taller, his height now almost at my chest.

"I'm here now. You don't have to hide anymore. You're going to come live at the palace."

"Yay! Yay! Yay!" Saad jumps up and down. Aya giggles and copies him.

He frowns, turning to me. "She copies everything I do. It's annoying!"

"She admires you." It's something I always wished I had with Nawaz, but had to stay silent. Now, that can change.

A woman comes into the room, then gasps and lowers her gaze when she sees me. "Apologies, I-I was just coming in to bathe them. I will return later—"

"No, stay." As much as I want to wrap them up and never let them out of my sight again, I know they're safe and cared for. I'll be back to tuck them in tonight and maybe I'll even tell them some of the stories from my time away—maybe I'll leave out the man that tried to torture Alara. "Do you know which room Alara has been placed in?"

"Who?"

"The girl who arrived with us. Brown eyes, wild curls."

"Oh she has just departed."

"To where?"

The lady shakes her head, looking concerned. "I'm sorry. I don't know."

"I'll come to see the kids later. Do what you must." With that, I'm out the room and running through the halls once again.

Outside, I push through the crowds that remain out-side—many have questions and some are just looking for a reason to cheer and celebrate.

My feet take me in the direction of Wadi, where I remember there is a hole in the mountain which she uses as a shortcut.

Her figure comes into view, her hair brushing behind her with the wind. My feet crunch against the sand.

It's a strange and unfamiliar feeling to be back on land; to have the sun beating down on my skin and warming me.

"Alara!"

She stops, spinning. I run until my boots are basically against hers. My breath is hard, my heart knocking against my chest.

"Hi." She steps back. She has been distant this whole time, and I couldn't figure out why. Now I see she was never planning on staying.

"You could have said goodbye."

Her cheeks redden, or maybe it's because she's no longer used to the sun. "I thought you'd stay up there with the kids. I didn't want to disturb."

"You're leaving?"

"Well, you've gotten everything you wanted." She sifts from side to side, nervously. "There's nothing left here for me here. I was just a nuisance that came in and threw everything upside down. I know my place."

"Not everything," I say. She looks at me with confusion, lines forming between her eyebrows. "I haven't gotten everything I want."

That makes her still.

I tuck her hair behind her ear. "But I'm about to." My head dips closer and my lips meet hers.

It's been a while since I've kissed her, and I craved it. Her soft lips, the little whimper she makes to let me know it feels good and, most of all, the feeling of knowing she is here and she wants me too.

She pulls away from the kiss and I involuntarily lean in. "There's nothing for me to do here. Do you expect me to sit around looking pretty?"

"You'd do a good job," I tease, still looking at her lips. She laughs and pushes my shoulder. "You do have a place. I need someone from Wadi, who knows the land and the ways that it can improve."

Her hand is still on my shoulder. "I can do that."

I shake my head, pressing my finger to her lips. "And, I want you to be by my side. You know, in case you get nightmares and I can protect you from big bad monsters like I always do." I grin from ear to ear, knowing that'll irritate her.

But it doesn't irritate her. She steps closer, so that her chest is against mine. "You want one night together?" she asks, knowing the implications of that.

That is far from what I want. I want her smile in the morning. I want her words of comfort when things get tough, which they will. I want her to be there to sit beside me when I read stories to Saad and Aya. I want her.

I crave to be with you forever.